Coffee Time Ki

And other Tales

(Including the Grufferty Letters)

By

Lyn Watts

Coffee Time Killer

And other Tales

(Including the Grufferty Letters)

First published March 2019

10 9 8 7 6 5 4 3 2 1 0

Copyright © Lyn Watts 2015, 2016. 2017 & 2018

ISBN 978-0-9932977-9-3

Printed by Print Domain, Thurnscoe, Rotherham, S63 0QZ

Published in England by: WattKnott Publishing, Testers, Whatlington, Battle TN33 0NS

www.wattknottpublishing.co.uk

Contents

Introduction

Alone   1

A Gentlemen's Home   6

The Wish   11

A Cleansing Tide   16

Mrs Crosby   22

The Blue Glove – an Arctic Mystery   30

Lost on the Moor   35

Inside Out   40

Living Memory   44

Old Flames   50

The Blue Idol of India   57

The Stairs   61

Second Time Around   67

Coffee Time Killer   71

The Old House   76

Vengeance   82

Martha of the Dell   88

The Glorious Few   93

Life's a Gamble   97

The Grufferty Letters   101

Grufferty Proposes a Toast   138

Introduction

Here is my third compilation of short stories. There are nineteen of them plus, in part two, the Grufferty Letters and Grufferty Proposes a Toast (both with fairly humble apologies to C. S. Lewis). Some of these have been published in Sussex, Kent and Dorset magazines while others have not been published at all. In each case the stories have been looked at afresh and, in many cases, altered, lengthened and edited. They vary from simple love stories to tales with a twist to supernatural happenings and general short story fiction designed to delight the reader. The historical tales involve much research and I strive to offer an accurate picture of how times would have been in any given time period.

Writing for magazines usually involves the discipline of writing to a word count. There are no such restrictions in a compilation such as this. I sincerely hope you enjoy reading them.

Lyn Watts February 2019

Alone

Becky threw the last things into the cases yelling at the girls to hurry as she went. She checked that the passports and tickets were in her bag for the umpteenth time, then took mental stock of the final jobs done. Milk cancelled, post diverted, Cat safely boarded with her neighbour.

"Hannah, Millie, get down here NOW!" She yelled at the girls, as the taxi driver rang the doorbell.

Cases safely stowed in the back, girls seatbelts fastened, at last they were off, on the long journey to the airport.

The thin wintery sun shone blindingly through the windows and the heater was turned right up, making the taxi swelteringly hot. The hum of the engine on the long drive was soporific so it wasn't long before both girls had fallen asleep each side of her, leaving Becky with her thoughts and fears for the journey ahead.

She had made great progress these last few months without Roger. Her worries and misery in those first few weeks had been unsurpassed. She had led a fairly sheltered life until then, a small exclusive school, doting parents, everything done for her. Her marriage to Roger had been a happy one, He was extremely capable and had managed all their finances, all legal paperwork when buying the house, managed all the bills etc. She had only ever had to concentrate on the cooking and cleaning, her part time job in the flower shop and, latterly, helping the girls with their reading after school and playgroup. Life had been a rose-coloured paradise until six months ago when, suddenly, Roger was gone and life turned upside down. For the sake of the two girls, Becky had been forced to get on with life. Her parents were the other side of the world now, living with her brother in Australia; so were unable to help. Hannah was six years old and Millie was four. Happily they loved their village school and nursery school respectively, and this had helped them to cope with losing their father.

Becky quickly found herself having to take responsibility for everyday things, totally on her own. Managing to set up a new direct debit for the first time felt like a major life achievement. Struggling alone to get the girls up and dropped off at school before dashing off to the shop and her work every morning was exhausting. Picking them up from school, cooking dinner, getting them off to bed, it was an endless lonely round of work. Then there were the lonely nights. These were the worst. The bed seemed vast and cold without Roger and she had trouble sleeping. Every noise made each fibre of her body tense and she would strain her ears to hear the cause. Checking and double checking the locks before going to bed and being alert for the girls waking as now she was alone in allaying their childish fears and solving their juvenile problems.

In the last few months when Roger was with them, life had been hellish for them all. Finances were at rock bottom. Becky had dreaded every letter through the letterbox and every knock at the door. Bill's piling up, many unable to be paid, the worry…. It had put a strain on their marriage too as Roger was worried and felt a completely irrational guilt. She sighed and looked down at Millie sleeping in her arms, her little pink mouth was slightly open and a strand of her light brown hair over her eyes. Becky brushed it gently back off her face and thought how lucky she was to have the girls. They had kept her going through all the worry and trauma. Well, she had the future to think of now and here they were arriving at the airport's South terminal.

She paid the taxi driver and ushered the girls through the check-in and finally they were in the departure lounge. Falling into a seat, Becky took stock. They had been so lucky to be given this new opportunity. Old fears had resurfaced when she heard about the journey they had to make. Panic had gripped her. The last time she had made a lengthy journey, to see her family in Australia, Roger had been with her to organise things and find passports, flight departure gates and all the other things she now had to do alone; but, somehow, she had managed it! A warm feeling of pride enveloped her. Yes, she had kept them all going this past six months. The house was still standing and all of the bills were paid. She had even managed to decorate the downstairs cloakroom and hallway. It had been hard work and worrying, but it had paid off.

Nearly there now, she thought, just the flight and then they would arrive in Dubai. The thought made her glow with happiness. The job offer had been a lifesaver for them even if it did mean Roger moving to Dubai, but now they would have a wonderful family holiday. She would see Roger and the girls would spend the school summer break with their daddy. Back home for just a few more months before he joined them for good; just in time for Easter, when he was to take up his new post in the company's UK branch. After his period of unemployment, Roger's new job had solved all their financial problems. The holiday, and transfer to the UK, were unexpected bonuses.

The boarding of their flight was announced.

"Come on girls!" said Becky, gathering her bags. "The last stage of the journey, in a few short hours we will see Daddy."

"Yay, daddy!" they cried, and they headed for the boarding gates.

A Gentleman's Home

Hetty walked across from the car park towards the entrance. She had long wanted to see Muchley Castle. The setting had stayed in her mind since childhood when she had stayed in the area on a family holiday with her parents some forty five years ago. The castle was sited on a hill, built from the most attractive weathered stone and with a backdrop of scenic countryside, it looked friendly, warm and homely despite its size and presence.

To her childish eyes it had looked like a typical castle from her book of fairy tales. She could imagine a beautiful princess sleeping the years away in it, awaiting her prince charming. The holiday had been over in a flash, they had only stayed in the area for a week and there hadn't been time to visit the castle. Years later, when Hetty was invited to holiday in the area with her son and his family she had jumped at the chance. She could babysit her grandsons in the evenings while Jake and Laura went out and she could spend quality time with them in the daytime.

By midweek, the children were demanding a day at the beach. Hetty was not good at sitting on sand for hours, so she suggested that she take herself to the castle for the day and they would all meet for dinner later. Hetty still needed some personal time occasionally. Jake's father had died some two years ago leaving her a widow whilst still in her early fifties. She had adjusted to life alone and was grateful for her son' presence and for having a loving family around her. Sometimes, she felt at her most lonely surrounded by kind people who meant well. She felt the need to get away on her own every so often.

The castle was open to the public from 10am so, after a late breakfast, she waved them all off to the beach and took herself off in her little blue Audi. As she walked from the car her stomach gave a leap of excitement. The castle looked exactly as she remembered it.

Hetty paid her entrance fee and paused in the great hall to look at the books on sale on a rack just inside the entrance. A thin volume entitled 'Ghosts of Muchley' caught her attention, and she was perusing this when a rich cultured voice said: "I wouldn't read that if you are on your own! It's scary!"

She looked up to see a distinguished looking gentleman of around sixty years old. He had silver grey hair swept back and his blue eyes twinkled with amusement. Hetty took in the casual tweed jacket with the leather patches at the elbows and mud splashed corduroy trousers. 'He must be a guide,' she thought to herself, but said: "I had no idea the castle was haunted!"

The grey haired gentleman proceeded to tell her the various stories of the hauntings in the castle. He spoke with great knowledge and authority and started to show her the haunted stairway.

Hetty found herself fascinated by the sound of his voice, fruity vowels and animated descriptions held her attention as he showed her from room to room. She felt a little guilty monopolising him as she felt sure he had other parties of visitors to attend to. He finished by inviting her to a ghost hunting evening at the castle.

"It is a fun evening with an hour long tour of the haunted sites then dinner in the great hall" he told her.

She thought it would be a good thing to spend some quality time on one of the evenings and leave the young family to themselves. It was only two nights away so she agreed to buy a ticket, but the gentleman wouldn't hear of it. "No! Please come as my guest!" He insisted, pressing a ticket into her hand.

When the evening came Hetty arrived at the castle and presented her ticket. There was no sign of her distinguished gentleman, she felt a little let down, but the tour was really interesting and the old castle worked it's magic on her so she felt a warm glow of pleasure just being there.

After the tour the party went into the hall for dinner, Hetty saw her gentleman friend sitting on the main table. He beckoned her over and held out the seat next to him for her to sit on. It occurred to her that she hadn't even asked him his name, nor had she told him hers. She opened her mouth to ask but was silenced by someone tinkling a glass and a footman announced:

"Pray silence for your host – Sir Peter Billington, Lord Muchley!" To Hetty's amazement (and embarrassment) her gentleman friend stood up to give his guests their welcoming speech!

The dinner was a huge success for Hetty, They had lots in common, a love for the countryside, a love of animals and both had lost much loved partners to illness. She found Peter such good company and so attentive that she agreed to spend the last day of the holiday with him so he could show her round the grounds and farm.

Hetty and Peter kept in contact after the holiday. She would visit some weekends; on others he would go to her house or they would stay in cosy country inns. Hetty's family get on really well with Peter's grown up family and her grandsons loved the castle.

They were married the following spring. Hetty still loves Muchley castle, but now she loves it's Lord too. The princess has at last been awoken by her handsome prince and they are living happily ever after in the castle!

The Wish

Lexie was lost. She knew it was her own fault for stomping off from her mummy and her baby brother in a temper as she had, but she was now afraid. Only five years old, she didn't know her way home even though she had been born and raised in the small run down seaside town.

She sat down and cried bitterly. It wasn't fair, she had set all her hopes on getting the pink Princess bike with the fairy wheels for Christmas. Now mummy had told her to choose something else as they simply couldn't afford it this year.

All her friends at her new infant school had bikes, just because her daddy had gone to heaven earlier this year, it didn't seem right that she should miss out. Lexie missed daddy, she loved mummy but mummy was often sad these days. Lexie buried her face in her hands and rocked backwards and forwards sobbing uncontrollably.

Sylvie stepped outside in the break to smoke a cigarette. What a way to make a living she thought to herself. Dressed up in a bleedin' tutu with a wand and crepe wings. Why didn't she listen at school? She could have been a nurse, or a teacher, helping people. Instead she followed her dreams of becoming famous. Now she was a second rate actress playing the fairy godmother in the touring company's production of Cinderella in this dead and alive seaside town!

The first performance started after Christmas in January. This was the final dress rehearsal before the Christmas break.

Sylvie looked across the green by the promenade opposite the theatre stage door. A little girl was crying her eyes out and she seemed to be all alone. Flicking her cigarette butt away, Sylvie strode across the road and approached her.

"Don't cry little one, what's wrong?" she asked her. Lexie just sobbed more and more. "Hey," Sylvie put her arms around her, "I'm Sylvie, what's your name?" Lexie looked up. "Lex, Lexie" she sobbed and gasped, then noticing Sylvie's dress, "Are you a fairy?"

Sylvie smiled, "Yes, I'm your fairy godmother and if you stop crying and tell me what's wrong I might grant you a wish!"

Lexie stopped crying. Turning a tearstained face towards Sylvie she blurted out the whole sorry story. She told how her daddy had gone to heaven earlier and how mummy had to care for her baby brother and her all alone. How she had desperately wanted the pink bike for Christmas more than anything, but mummy couldn't afford it and how she had stomped off in a fit of pique and was now lost. At this point the bottom lip quavered and her eyes filled with tears again.

"Well don't cry" said Sylvie, The first problem we can remedy easily, come on, we'll go and find your mummy". She took Lexie's hand and led her across the gardens to the edge of the promenade. "As for the second wish, be a very good girl from now on, don't run away from Mummy again and we will see what we can do. Close your eyes and make a wish before you go to sleep each night". As they walked they spied Lexie's mum, complete with pushchair, looking distraught and calling for her with rising hysteria.

"Off you go sweetie!" said Sylvie releasing Lexie's hand. Then becoming conscious of her costume she turned and ran back through the stage door. "Mummy, mummy" cried Lexie and threw herself into her mother's arms. "Oh Lexie! Where have you been? I was so worried." Lexie explained that she had met a fairy godmother who had shiny wings and she had found them for her. Her mother was amused at her childish imagination as they walked home.

Kelly was growing greedy, trying to persuade Darren to cut corners on his ingredients and to push up the prices of their meals. Darren prided himself on his cooking so many rows ensued between them.

In all the whirl of success, they had never got round to moving bedrooms and were still sleeping in the front bedroom.

One night they had a huge row just as they were closing up for the night. Darren angrily told her how greedy she was becoming, causing Kelly to run out to the beach in the harbour, slamming the door behind her. Sitting, sobbing on the beach, she suddenly felt paralysed. She couldn't move her arms or legs, she couldn't even cry out. All she could do was watch the distant shoreline by moonlight as the tide slowly engulfed her, filling her nostrils with water.

In the early morning, Darren found her body. It was taken back to the pub and laid on their bed until the coroner could be summoned.

Darren sold up and moved away. He had a very generous offer from Mr Enfield's eldest daughter and her husband, who had to earn their own living now that her parents fortunes had dwindled somewhat.

Straight away they decided they could not sleep in the front bedroom after Kelly's body had been laid there, so they redecorated the back room. The pub name was changed back to The Royal George and it offered good wholesome pub food at reasonable prices.

It became a huge success with locals and visitors alike, and the new owners slept soundly.

Mrs Crosby

Steve put his phone back into his pocket, he felt his throat tighten and tears were pricking his eyes. It was always good to hear from his best friend Roger, they spoke on the phone weekly, but this time Rog had some bad news.

They had known each other from the age of five, when both had started at Brookland Primary school, the little village school near New Romney. Roger's mum, Mrs Crosby, was the headmistress there but Steve and Roger had started in the infants' class taught by Mrs Beany. At the age of seven Roger had been sent off to a posh boy's boarding school as it was considered unethical for his own mum to teach him. She could, however, teach Steve and Steve loved her sense of fun and the way she instilled a sense of pride in him. He felt he would be letting her down if he didn't deliver his best. Roger came home at school holidays and some weekends so that, even when Steve went up to 'big school', some twenty six years previously, they had remained firm friends.

Roger went onto study law and qualified as a solicitor. Steve gained an apprenticeship with Harvard Locks as a locksmith. When he was eighteen, just two years into his apprenticeship, his parents were killed by a jack-knifing lorry on the A2. Mrs Crosby was asked by the police to break the news to him and, as a result of her kindness, she became like a surrogate mum. He stayed at the Crosby's house every holiday and, when his work brought him to Kent (he would travel all over the South East with his work). When he became a fully-fledged locksmith he married his long-term girlfriend, Alice. Mrs Crosby stood in for mum at the wedding and Roger was the best man. The couple settled down in suburban South London and they had two children, Rob and Emma.

Roger had set up his own practice in Hythe, married Emily and they had Charlotte and Ben. The families kept in touch. Roger and Steve would meet up for the odd football match or travel to the races at Folkstone. Sometimes Emily would cook Sunday lunch for them all - Steve and Alice would drive down for the day, stopping off for a cuppa with Mrs Crosby on the way home. Steve had never forgotten her kindness and she was just like his mum when he needed advice, She had a code she lived by – 'always stay true to your principles and it will work out right in the end.' This was her motto and she instilled it into Steve.

He could barely take in what Roger had told him. Mrs Crosby had died. Steve knew that she had suffered with heart problems for the previous few years. After the death of Mr Crosby, she had moved into the granny annexe of Emily and Roger's fine big house so as to be near enough to help should she need it. Emily had taken morning tea into the annexe that morning and found her peaceful, composed but quite dead and cold. Steve took the news very hard. It was, he thought, the final straw in a series of bad - no, terrible - disasters to befall him and Alice.

Firstly Alice had found a lump in her right breast. Thankfully it was treatable but surgery and radiotherapy had made her feel very sick. Caring for the children and house was more than enough for her to cope with. They decided that they could manage on one salary for a while. Alice gave up her part time job in an estate agent. But then government cut-backs and the recession had an effect on even a big company like Harvard Locks. Redundancies had to be made and Steve was one of the casualties. There was absolutely nothing on the jobs front for him. He applied for dozens - even unsuitable ones - but no one wanted a thirty seven year old with few skills except some basic woodwork and a good knowledge of locks. The redundancy pay, such as it was, had almost gone and the jobseekers allowance just about prevented them from starving. There was no choice but to put their house on the market. They had very little equity in the small semi, but they did have a large mortgage to pay, so that, at least, would be finished and they could find a flat the size of a shoebox to rent. Then, one day as he was leaving the jobcentre, he was approached by a dark haired furtive little man with a swarthy complexion and an East London accent.

"'Scuse me mate" said the man "did I 'ear that you know a fing or two about locks?" Steve affirmed his skills, "'Ow would you like to earn a couple of grand for a nights work? A mate of mine is 'avin a bit a trouble wiv a safe and if you can crack it for us - no questions asked, like - there's two grand in it for you."

Steve must have shown shock on his face as the swarthy man looked conspiratorial, and said, soothingly:

"Take a day or two to fink it over, 'ere's me number; name's Jon Smith."

With that he passed Steve a scrap of paper with a mobile phone number scrawled on it. He gave a cheeky wink and walked off. Steve thought about it all the way home. At first he dismissed it. It was totally against his upbringing and principles. More importantly it went against everything his parents (and Mrs Crosby) had taught him. But he and Alice were in a desperate situation. Emma had her tenth birthday

coming up soon and was hoping for a laptop. Rob needed new football boots for school. Playing straight and honest in life had got him nowhere; two grand would solve a lot of their immediate problems. He hadn't exactly been told it was illegal; it could be the guy's safe was stuck and he needed it fixed. Hell, he thought, he would do it. After all, he was only doing what was best for his family and helping someone else out. Wasn't that what a father did?

But he knew deep inside that this was not the way! He had almost rung the number that very afternoon, but then Roger had told him about Mrs Crosby. This brought Steve up short. What would she have said if she had known his intentions? How could he face Roger and Emily or Alice and the kids, for that matter? He decided to put the whole thing out of his mind for a day or two. He had a funeral to attend.

Steve had just enough money for the train and bus tickets and could get to the funeral. Alice and the kids could not attend. Alice was not feeling up to the journey and the children had school.

It was a beautiful day with a blue sky, the marshes looked clear and smoothly flat. It made Steve realise how much he loved and missed the area. The thought that the family could soon be renting a grim basement flat in London made his heart ache almost as much as the loss of Mrs Crosby.

The church was packed with people and flowers, many tributes from old pupils from past years. She and Mr Crosby had chosen a double plot in Brookland churchyard - the village they had both loved. After the service most of the congregation repaired to the village pub where a running buffet had been provided.

"You remember David Matfield?" said Roger, leading a short, chubby smiling man with receding hair up to Steve. "He runs his own building firm now".

Steve remembered a cheerful kid from the village school who's Dad had been the local builder.

"Hi Steve, good to see you again." He said. "Roger tells me you can fit doors and skirting boards and that you are a master locksmith now".

"Well, I was, David!" replied Steve, "I got made redundant last year and nothing doing on the job front since then."

"Well now", said David "My firm has just won the contract from the council to build the houses for the local affordable-housing scheme. We are inundated with improvement work too, as folk can't move with the property slump, so they are extending instead. I need a good locksmith who can also help out the chippy with the woodworking from time to time, how would you fancy working for me?"

"I'd be delighted, but I live in London – I mean, what are the rental prices like here?" blustered Steve.

Roger had been standing behind Steve eavesdropping, he now placed a brotherly arm round his shoulders; "Look, Steve, when dad died, mum couldn't manage but didn't want to leave the school house. You remember they bought it from the Education Authority when she retired. She only agreed to move into our annexe if we kept the house on for her. We had intended to sell after her death, but couldn't bear to part with it. We don't need to sell, so we thought we might rent it out. We would need to find good, reliable tenants who would love and care for the place and who we could trust, what about it Steve? You, Alice and the children? I'll make sure the rent is within your budget and if your situation improves later, you can have first refusal when we do sell. What do you think?"

Steve felt sandbagged! Waves of relief and gratitude washed over him, interspersed with a sense of joy and excitement. Tears pricked his eyes and he could hardly trust his own voice when he said "Sounds a perfect arrangement, Thank you both! I will, of course need to run it past Alice, but I know she loves Brookland as much as I do and the kids love the countryside, can I ring you both tomorrow morning?"

As he felt in his pocket for his train ticket on the way home, Steve pulled out the scrap of paper with the swarthy man's number on it. He tore it into shreds and threw it in the bin in the station waiting room. Later as he dozed on the train going back to London, Steve dreamed that Mrs Crosby was sitting with him, as she had many times after the death of his parents. She was smiling – "Didn't I tell you, always stay true to your principles and it will work out right in the end!"

The Blue Glove, an Arctic Mystery

The minibus trundled the miles away. The Icelandic landscape was almost lunar in appearance, yet it had its own beauty. I loved the country. I always felt well here and the climate seemed to suit me. Sadly I could only visit for holidays as my work in England kept me busy for the rest of the year.

I had done the usual tours - Golden Circle, volcanoes, Blue Lagoon etc. but this year I took a small minibus day tour to Gullfoss, the amazing waterfall, Myrdalsjökull Glacier and Reynisfjara beach below Vik on the South coast.

Stefan, our driver, picked me up from my hotel in downtown Reykjavik and stopped to collect all the other tourists from their hotels or apartments. I was gratified to see all eight seats were full on the bus as we motored towards Gullfoss, for our first stop - and with a welcome kiosk to get a warm coffee.

I usually visited Iceland in late February or early March as there was still sufficient snow to make it seem wintery but, if you were very lucky, there was some sunshine and blue sky to lift the spirits. Today was one of those days. The bus was warm and we were able to undo our thick thermal jackets. I sat next to a charming lady, Sarah, a few years younger than myself, who turned out to be a veterinary surgeon. Behind us were a couple in their sixties from the USA. A Japanese couple and their adult son sat on the back three seats. Next to Stefan in the single right hand front seat was a quiet gentleman who held his rucksack and camera on his lap the whole time and spoke to no one, not even the gregarious Stefan.

I had failed to notice where he had got on. He looked very serious and didn't return the smile of greeting that we all gave each other as we alighted at Gullfoss. I had visited Gullfoss on a previous Golden Circle tour. It was the biggest waterfall in Iceland and certainly one of the most impressive. After our coffee, we wandered around the falls and took photographs. The quiet man just stood in wonder and stared intently at the waterfall and the rainbow glowing distinctly behind it.

The American couple asked us to photograph them with their camera then did the same for Sarah and myself. I admired the troll crossing - a tiny house built into the side of the road just as you approached the car park. Stefan explained that belief in trolls was still prevalent in Iceland and the little houses were built as a mark of respect for them.

We drove on to Myrdalsjökull Glacier. Stefan warned us all about the dangers of walking alone on the glacier. He told us that about 11% of Iceland's land area is covered by glaciers. They are constantly shifting and moving and they supply the freshest and most pure drinking water in the world. The knowledgeable Stefan took mine and Sarah's water bottles and stooped by a stream to fill them for us. It was the best water I have ever tasted.

Stefan took us for a little walk just onto the first part of the glacier.

"You need a proper guided tour and snow shoes to walk the glacier properly." He told us. "Never wander away from your guide; the section you are standing on may not be here tomorrow!"

Behind him I noticed the quiet man walking away from us as if in a daze. I grabbed Stefan's elbow and pointed him out imploring Stefan to call him back. He nodded to me and went to call the American couple back from the edge of a crevasse in the ice. As Sarah and I walked past the crevasse, I looked down and noticed the quiet man had dropped one of his distinctive blue woollen gloves several feet down it. I wondered if his hands would get too cold before the end of the day.

We got back on the bus and headed to Vik for a late lunch at the diner. I was concerned to see that the quiet man had not returned to the minibus with the group. Stefan had apparently done a head count before we left Myrdalsjökull. I told him that the man was missing, but he merely smiled and stated:

"No, all seven are present and correct."

When I protested he insisted that the seat next to him had been vacant all journey. Sarah didn't seem to know who I was talking about either. I began to think I was losing my sanity!

I felt a mild unease for the rest of the day, which took the edge off my appetite at the Vik diner. I rallied at the beautiful Reynisfjara beach with its black sand and breath taking basalt rock formations, which was our afternoon treat.

The thin watery sun was beginning to fade as we boarded the minibus for our homeward journey. It was past 5pm and it had been a full day. The bus was warm and soon Sarah fell asleep. Stefan beckoned me to come and sit by him in the front.

He told me the stories of the glaciers. He told of Vatnajökull glacier in Skaftafell National park and how Tŏmas

Tömasson and his daughter Sigriour Tŏmasdottir had fought to save it for the nation.

I told him how worried I was for the quiet man and he became serious and looked concerned. The sky was dark now and most of the others were sleeping or reading. He leant towards me.

"Some ten years ago" he began in a hushed voice, "we had a gentleman on the tour who was travelling alone. He would not stay with the rest of the party and my predecessor only just prevented him from walking behind the fall at Gullfoss. That would have been extremely dangerous at that time of the year. He wandered off at Myrdalsjökull and nobody noticed. He was never found. It was thought he had committed suicide. Only his blue glove was found which can be seen to this day in the crevasse near the edge of the glacier - you may have noticed it as we passed. In those days we only had the walking guided tours, so he must have walked a long way off."

He saw my pallor and look of horror. "Don't worry!" he said "He'll be okay, the Trolls will be caring for him now!"

Lost on the Moor

I was born too early. I knew that because everyone remarked about it being a hard world for such a small vulnerable one. It was a vast and exciting world though, and I was much loved by my mother and her large family. Always curious and inquisitive by nature, I found the moor where we lived totally fascinating and absorbing. Days flew by as I played with my friends and explored. I was well behaved. I always listened to my mother and stayed fairly close to home - security, plenty of food, warmth and love - until that fateful day.

It had started as usual; pottering about, playing with my friends. I became curious to know what lay beyond the boundaries of our small farmstead. I was with my friend Dave and we wandered a little further away from the others that day. I noticed the grass, how pretty it looked with the thick white frost glistening in the weak wintry sun. I remarked to Dave how the farmhouse looked black against the pale white wintry sky, while what little sun there was seemed determined to keep hiding behind the solid white clouds. The day was bleak with clouds; a vast heavy canopy of paleness above and a white carpet of frost which crunched under our feet. We started playing hide and seek. Dave was easy to spot as he had no idea of camouflage. I, laughing, ran farther away, hiding behind the trees. Plop! A small nut fell in front of me, looking up I spotted a small grey squirrel. I called softly to him and he hopped down and grabbed the nut from the hard grass, stuffing it into his cheek before flattening himself against the tree trunk. I watched in amusement as he suddenly rushed up the trunk to the next branch, then helter skelter across to the next branch, stuffing nuts into his cheeks as he went. This amused me so much I had to try to follow, but of course, I couldn't climb the tree trunk! I heard a furious cawing from above, a clump of crows nests showed black against the sky, their occupants scolding me furiously. I decided I had better leave them to it, Just then a large rabbit loped by with a mouthful of dandelion leaves, he watched me warily. I decided to follow him, to see if he could lead me to a really good hiding place where Dave would never think to look. He ran, paused, ate a little, ran on and repeated this several times until he finally disappeared down a hole in the grassy bank. It was far too small a hole for me to follow. Oh well, I thought, I'd better let Dave find me; but, as I looked around, everything seemed strange. There was no sign nor sound of Dave or the others. I had absolutely no idea where I was and, to make matters worse, big soft flakes of snow brushed my cheeks and eyelashes, settling on my head and shoulders. I called, no reply came from anyone. I called again and again struggling to contain the panic which was rising and threatening to engulf me. Stay calm, I told myself, retrace your steps. But I had been so intent on what my bunny friend had been up to that I had absolutely no idea which direction I had come from. To make matters worse the snow was blanketing the landscape, masking any familiar landmarks there may have been. I looked frantically for the farmhouse, but I could see only trees around me. A cold fear gripped me and a huge knot formed in my stomach. I had a lump in my throat and felt sick. Dusk was beginning to close in and still I wandered, calling and calling in vain.

After a while I felt quite dizzy with the cold, and the whiteness of the world I found myself in. I was hungry too, I lay down under a tree, I had been crying and calling for hours now it seemed. All to no avail, I needed a rest. I closed my eyes, but some very disturbing dreams made rest impossible. I dreamed I was being pelted with nuts by a giant squirrel while a rookery of crows screeched at me and a giant rabbit led me deeper and deeper into a forest of ice. I woke with a start. I felt stiff, cold, hungry and very much alone. I wanted my mother. I tried to call again but my voice was hoarse with calling. I missed the others too. I thought of my home, warmth, cosy comfort and my cousins and friends. Would I ever see them again? I missed them all, but most of all I missed my mother. Here I was, cold and afraid in a strange white world with no idea whatsoever as to how to get home. Would I die here? Would death be painful? What lay beyond death? My mother had always warned me about wandering off on my own and now I knew why and I wished I had remembered her warnings and heeded them. I felt so sorry for myself stuck alone in the midst of a blizzard. I was crying so pitifully that I failed to notice the big dog that crept up on me sniffing the ground. He stopped with a paw raised and barked. It made me jump and I was a little afraid. He stood there barking and wouldn't leave my side. He looked kind and his breath was warm as he sniffed me. I saw a pair of long boots and breeches, looking up I saw the man.

"Come on little one," he said "you're safe now."
He scooped me up into his strong arms and wrapped a coat around me. I felt a little afraid of him. I didn't know who he was, we were miles from home in the dark and snow, but he was warm and the coat smelt very comforting.

The man loaded me into his Land Rover, where the dog was already wagging his tail with his great silly head out of the window. It was warm and cosy in the cab with the coat over me, so I soon fell asleep. Presently, we pulled up outside a familiar building. I could hear my friends calling. I heard Dave's voice; then, wonder of wonders, I heard my dear mother's voice calling me. The man carried me into the barn and set me down.

"Mum. Oh mum! I have missed you!" I cried, "I'm so sorry I wandered off, I will never ever do that again."

She nuzzled me with her warm woolly nose. "You're home now George, my little one." she said "You are lucky that Gyp, the collie, found you and alerted the shepherd. You are a very silly, but a very lucky, little lamb!" I had to agree with that.

"Baaaaaa!" I said.

Inside Out

She looked at the woman in the mirror. She saw her every day; always so confident, elegant and capable. Her world looked exactly like her own, but, somehow, much better - more vibrant and inviting; better than her own dull life, with her apprehension at facing each day.

The Mirror Woman was a successful woman – independent; a lecturer and author, specialist in her own subject. She had a big house, a successful husband, three beautiful children and everything to live for, whereas Demi felt cramped, full of doubt, and lacked confidence in everything she did. Her husband - she was sure he didn't love her. He stayed with her for appearances sake. That was what Demi thought. He often stayed away on business, or worked late in the office. At times she thought his P.A. saw more of him than she did. Their love life was virtually non-existent. He was so tired when he was home and, often she had to leave very early to get to the next lecturing venue. The Mirror Woman, had everything, she looked as though she oozed fulfilment in every way; a loving, devoted husband, her children studying for glittering careers in their chosen professions. Demi's children were ordinary, with normal youthful uncertainties. The eldest had just started University, but was finding the foundation degree in history a struggle. The middle child couldn't decide between studying law or music, and she was convinced that her youngest was getting mixed up with the wrong crowd at sixth form college - she was sure she had smelt cannabis on him when he got home the other evening (or rather the early hours of the morning!)

Demi had worries about her own career; that people would tire of her lectures - she was, after all, not getting any younger. It became more and more of a struggle keeping up with the latest research to stay at the top of her chosen tree, and the writing seemed to take a back seat to all of her other commitments. How long was it since she'd had an article published in the professional journal that had launched her lecture career? How long since she had undertaken a new research project? The Mirror Woman was always on top form - people hanging on her every word, the under-graduates always vying for her attention after lectures, the post graduates aspiring to be like her. Whereas Demi often felt too shy to face them after lectures and rushed off gathering up her notes and muttering of previous engagements.

Demi looked at her face in the mirror. Her hair was becoming dull and losing its brilliance and shine; and there were more greys than she felt happy with. The crinkles in the corners of her eyes had turned to wrinkles, as had the deep lines on her top lip. She had to spend more and more on cosmetics and hairdressing appointments, whereas the Mirror Woman looked as though she had it all naturally, waking up and instantly looking wonderful, fresh and vibrant. Why couldn't she feel and be like the Mirror Woman?

Demi took a quick mental review of her life. A treadmill; rushing here and there and what did she really know of the anxieties her children faced? What interest did she show in her husband's business? The last twenty years had been spent juggling! Juggling her career, childbirth, then raising her three children; the worries about childcare when the children were too sick for nursery school; juggling her own diary to support her husband at the important business dinners (some of which she had been obliged to miss due to her own career commitments) panicking when her cleaner left and the house became a mess. She thought of the state-of- the- art kitchen that had cost a small fortune but that only ever saw real food cooked at the weekend (and only then if her husband wasn't eating at the golf club). Midweek, they made do with 'ready meals' or ate at their respective, separate official work functions.

The Mirror Woman looked as though she swept through life with ease; a glittering social life and a perfect family life. As Demi watched her, the Mirror Woman's husband approached her from behind and wrapped his arms around her shoulders.

Kissing the nape of her neck he said "Come on! You look wonderful as always. I know I've been busy lately, and so have you but, we need time out. You have been too introspective lately. I know you have been riddled with self-doubt and a little depressed so I have booked us a week away. A family winter holiday in Norway chasing the Northern lights suit you?"

He laid his chin on her shoulder and whispered: "I have missed you - we all have. We need some 'us' time together. I hate sharing you all the time with your adoring students." He kissed her ear.

It was at that point that Demi knew that she could break out of her brittle glass shell at any time and become the Mirror Woman in reality. Turning away from the mirror towards her husband she led him from the room by his hand.

"Show me the brochures!" she said with a smile. As they closed the door behind them the woman inside the mirror disappeared!

Living Memory

I really love this part of the world, the West Country, where I was brought up. Today, however, I was not very happy. I was driving along a typical Devon lane - narrow and with high hedges on each side. I dreaded meeting another vehicle as passing places were few and far between. Suddenly my temperature gauge started to rise. Damn! Just what I needed! There was nowhere to pull off the road safely. Then, just around the next bend, was a farm gate. I swung the car into the yard and stopped the engine. As I opened the bonnet, steam came gushing out at me.

"Dear, Oh dear!" said a voice. It was then that I noticed the lady tending a vegetable patch. She straightened as she addressed me. Behind her was a small cob cottage and a green hillside dotted with sheep. I explained my predicament.

"Well, my dear! You had best come inside while we ring Mallock!" and, signalling with her head towards the house, she set off with me trailing along behind her.

"Kettle on Peggy, we have a visitor!" she called as she headed straight for the telephone in the hallway. An older woman was standing at the black kitchen range. She motioned me towards a large pine table and said

"Sit yourself down, m'dear! We'm soon 'ave the tea brewed! You 'ave sugar, m'dear?"

Peggy had a broad Devon accent, unlike my friend, currently on the telephone. I sat and looked around the kitchen. I noticed that nothing appeared to have changed for years. The whole place looked stuck in time. As I mused, the first woman came back from the telephone.

"Mallock will come and sort you out, but he can't be here for another half hour or so, so you may as well have some cake with your tea."

Peggy chuckled "Mallock's half an hour… you make yourself comfortable M'dear, me and Joan, we don't get many visitors 'ere so we shan't mind a bit of a jaw!" Mallock ran the local garage and could turn his hand to most odd jobs, it seemed.

Peggy poured the tea and they served beautiful homemade scones with thick clotted cream and slices of sponge cake so light that it melted in the mouth. As I ate my cake they told me their story.

Joan had been evacuated from London during the war with her little boy Patrick. Her husband had been in the

RAF. Peggy had lost her husband many years previously at Paschendale and she had run the farm alone for a while, before Joan arrived.

It occurred to me that they must be a lot older than they looked as this was the 1970's. The West Country air must be good for the complexion, I thought.

Joan had found that she took to farming really quickly and soon she and Peggy had become firm friends, running the farm between them.

"'Corse in them days we didn't 'ave so many sheep" Peggy explained. "Much of the land 'ad to be turned to crops see, the government, ee don't allow us no waste, so we growed a lot more 'n we do now."

The war had ground on and, sadly, one day Joan had received news of her husband's death. She threw herself more and more into the farm and Peggy was grateful to her for making a huge success of the place. Patrick had been very young when his father went to war, so he wasn't so badly affected by his loss. Joan was devastated but found solace in the friendly locals and Peggy's stoicism. Both being widowed by war, the women found they had much in common.

Peggy had offered Joan and Patrick a permanent home with her, and Joan gratefully accepted. They had been firm friends ever since.

"Patrick is in the Navy now." said Joan, "Stationed at Plymouth, so we see a bit of him when he is home"

I told them about my plans to retire to the West Country. How I was dreadfully fed up with the rat race in London. I wanted a smallholding. We were interrupted by the sound of tyres on gravel.

"There's Mallock now!" said Joan jumping up. "Not bad for him, only an hour and a half!" Where had that time gone, I wondered. It had flown by talking to those charming ladies.

I went outside to explain to Mallock what had happened. It turned out to be a split hose on my radiator and he was able to repair it quite quickly. Joan brought out jugs of water to refill the system and I was pleasantly pleased at the incredibly cheap price asked for the call-out.

I took my leave of the ladies, thanking them once again for their generous hospitality and help and set off again for the area of my property search.

I then spent a few days fruitlessly searching for my retirement smallholding. It occurred to me that I was looking for somewhere just like the farmstead that Joan and Peggy had. As I set off for home I decided, on a whim, to buy them some flowers by way of thanks and to deliver them on my way past.

I drove down the lane and pulled into the farm gate. To my amazement the familiar vegetable patch was gone! The little cottage was covered in scaffolding and builders vans cluttered the yard. There were no sheep on the hillside above the cottage. I jumped out of the car.

"Where are the ladies?" I asked the first man I saw. He looked puzzled and called over an older man.

"'Ere! Dad! Lady 'ere asking for Mrs Lawson." The older man looked at me strangely. "Who wants to know?" he asked. When I told him I wanted to thank her for some help she had given me he continued: "Joan Lawson? 'Er died some three months ago!" He caught me as I swayed in a faint!

We sat on the low stone wall while he told me the story. It seemed old Peggy had died some fifteen years ago, leaving the farm to Joan. She had stayed on running it as best she could but as age crept on she could do less. The house badly needed modernising. She had died some twelve weeks earlier leaving the farm to Patrick her son. He had no need of it, as his naval career took him all over the world.

This local building firm had been hired by him to repair and restore the cottage and bring it up to date. Then he was to sell the whole farmstead.

Suddenly, without a shadow of a doubt I knew I had to buy it. I couldn't explain how I could possibly have met those ladies, but I knew that it was meant to be. I would be very happy here. I knew Peggy and Joan would approve. The builder gave me Patrick's number.

My journey home could wait for a few more hours. The local pub had a telephone and I would ring Patrick while my lunch was being prepared. It seemed that I was home at last!

Old Flames

I love this little church - All Saints at Iden; come to think of it I love Iden itself. It has been a salvation for me, a healing balm; the soothing oil on the troubled waters pf my life. I was born just a couple miles from here in the ancient town of Rye, where I lived with my parents and attended the little Church of England School and then the Community College. My parents travelled a great deal as my father's work took him all around the country, so I spent a considerable amount of time with my grandparents in their pretty old cottage in Iden village. I was extremely fond of both my grandparents and the dear little cottage they lived in, but the biggest attraction for me was Josh Funnell. Josh was two years above me at Rye College. A tall athletic boy, he excelled at sports and yet was highly intelligent too. He eventually became head boy, but I am getting ahead of myself.

Josh lived in the village too. He played guitar in the local youth club band, captained the junior cricket team and was so gorgeous that he held the hearts of every female in the district in the palm of his hand. Dark curly hair framed a square jaw and deep violet blue eyes that looked right into your soul. He could have any girl he chose. I was a fairly small, unremarkable girl; freckled and rather pale and pasty. He never seemed to notice me. Of course, he would say Hello when he saw me in the village, then smile at me in the school corridors if our paths crossed but he didn't give me a second glance. I, on the other hand, was smitten. My silent adoration from afar became almost an obsession when, quite by chance, he became my knight in shining armour one day.

Granddad had a small field of about an acre and a half with the cottage. For my tenth birthday they had bought me Pepper, a small, bay, Exmoor pony whom I adored as only a young girl can. He lived in my grandparent's field, but even when I wasn't staying with them I was riding him at least three times a week. One day I was riding Pepper through the village at a time when the village High Street was being repaired. As I rode around the bend a pneumatic road drill started. Pepper was a very quiet pony, but it caught us both unawares. He startled and bucked, spinning round and dashing off in the opposite direction! I came a cropper in the middle of the road. I was slightly stunned for a couple of seconds then I jumped up and ran after Pepper, tears of fright and anguish pouring down my face, blood pouring from the knee of my torn riding breeches and limping from a twisted ankle. As I ran up the road to the church, calling for Pepper, I came face to face with Josh.

He was holding Pepper by the bridle and stroking his nose talking soothingly to him all the while. His magnetism extended to horses apparently because Pepper was puffing slightly but had calmed and was making a gentle whickering noise in his throat. When Josh saw me he looked most concerned. "Poor Kat," he said, "Are you okay? Come on, I'll take you home." He led Pepper and placed his other arm around my shoulders leading us both back to my grandparents cottage. Despite my sore knee and ankle I was in heaven, but must have seemed like an idiot as I couldn't think of a word to say. I was totally unable make any attempt at conversation, and answered his concerned questions monosyllabically. Once he had handed me over to my concerned grandma, he untacked and brushed Pepper himself before leading him into his field, then, with a final expression of concern for my recovery, he was gone. That was it! I was devoted to him but from afar. He was always surrounded by both male friends and female admirers, he seemed to have a different girlfriend every week. I could only daydream and fantasise about how it would be to date him, to kiss him, the memory of how it felt to have his arm around me, sustained me for the next few months. I was, in my childish way, head over heels in love for the first time!

He left school when he turned eighteen (and I only sixteen). I heard that he had gone to university and then studied veterinary medicine. I went to the Agricultural College in Kent and took a National Diploma in Equine studies. Years passed. I went to work on a Stud farm in Hampshire and soon worked my way up into management. My grandparents kept me up to date with the local news. I heard that Josh had specialised in horses too and was the senior partner in a large equine practice in Kent. I was infatuated with a widowed Irish racehorse trainer who visited the stud farm regularly. He was several years older than I and had the gift of the gab and the Celtic charm that some of his kind are blessed with. I was impressed with the idea of being his wife. In reality our marriage was miserable. He turned out to be a bully and a heavy drinker. When I returned from a trip to my parents one weekend I found him in our bed with one of the stable girls. The mother of all rows blew up and the upshot was that he slapped me so hard that I had a black eye and a split lip! Meek and mild I may be, but I am not a doormat. One violent episode is one too many. I picked up my cases and returned to my parents. The only contact we had after that was through our solicitors!

My divorce settlement provided me with enough money to buy some twenty acres and ten stables just outside Rye. There was no living accommodation with the yard but I could stay at my parents, or in the small caravan I used as an office and day accommodation. I made an adequate living with my livery yard, and threw myself into teaching riding and caring for the horses. Every so often I would think of Josh and allow myself a little fantasy as to how it would be to be his wife. What a team we would have made - he with his equine health knowledge and I, with my stable management skills.

My life has been my horses and my yard for some five years now. I will be forty next month. My grandma had died some months ago and I was here in Iden churchyard visiting her grave when my heart gave a thump! I could recognise that blue/black hair and stature anywhere! Placing flowers on the grave of his grandparents was Josh. I caught my breath and mentally checked my appearance. I was in old jodhpurs with muddy knee length chaps and a rather bobbly fleece jacket. Before I could jump back behind a tree he spotted me. " Little Kat!" he said "How lovely to see you, I heard you were back and running your own yard." I felt my cheeks burn and my voice sounded like a croak to me "Good to see you, Josh." I said "How's the practice?" We walked and talked then sat on a flat gravestone by the church door and talked some more. I was surprised at how easy I felt in his company. He told me that he had never married (which amazed me, as he had enjoyed his pick of the most stunning girls). "I found most of them too superficial and shallow." He told me. "Beauty is really only skin deep, beautiful minds are far more precious and rare."

I found myself telling him about my failed marriage to my abusive ex-husband Words flowed very easily and, despite my adoration of him, I felt very comfortable in his presence. He clearly felt the same because he asked me if I would like to go to the local riding club Ball with him on the Saturday if he could manage to buy two tickets.

That was nine months ago. We moved together into the Georgian house that he had been renovating three months ago, and are getting married today. We are having a blessing in All Saints Church here in Iden after the registry office and I have never seen the place looking lovelier. That is what Josh told me about my appearance today! It seems he has always admired my peace and serenity, my way with horses and even my freckles. I have always loved him and I secretly knew we should (and would) be together one day. "I was waiting just for you!" my gorgeous new husband told me as we climbed into our waiting horse drawn carriage to whisk us away to the reception. "I was waiting for you to rescue me again." I said and smiled to myself as I threw my bouquet over my shoulder.

The Blue Idol of India

I still couldn't quite believe how easily I had won her. Watching her sleeping, she was still a very attractive woman. She had been a beauty but even in the soft greenish glow of the hotel night light, she looked her age now. The fine lines around her eyes and lips gave it away. I was sure she had undergone some cosmetic surgery. She could afford it. Some twenty years my senior, she was the extremely wealthy widow of a famous shipping magnet. On his death she had inherited his business empire, properties and the necklace he had commissioned to be made for her containing the exquisite and famous Blue Idol of India, one of the world's most precious blue diamonds.

When I heard she was coming here, it was easy to find out which hotel she would be staying at. I had long admired her and one of my ambitions was to see the famous diamond. I have been a lifelong admirer of precious stones, also an admirer of her beauty, in her younger days of course.

Now I am a fairly good looking guy, I keep myself fit and am well educated, Marlborough and Oxford, although I was a scholarship boy. Knowing she would be taking a suite here at the Randolph, I borrowed a couple of grand from an old chum, bought a new set of clothes and booked myself in. It was a simple matter to chat her up over pre dinner drinks and eventually I was invited up to her suite, where I have been sleeping, in the loosest sense of the word for most of her stay.

We have been getting on famously, I pride myself on my technique with the ladies and she was a very willing partner. She spoke of a long term relationship, perhaps taking me with her when she moved on to her next business appointments and then to one of her island homes. Her minders, all got to know me and she and I had very quickly become known as an item. That was what saved me in the events that were to follow.

About four one morning, we were woken by one of her bodyguards who keep watch outside her bedroom. Apparently, the necklace was kept in the safe in her sitting room area, just beyond the dressing room outside her bedroom. One of her entourage stays in the sitting room all night. This man was chloroformed silently and the safe opened. The necklace was missing!

The man minding the safe swore that it was me who had walked in, bold as brass, had said "goodnight" calling him by name, then, heading toward the dressing room, had suddenly swung round and pressed a chloroform pad over his nose and mouth. When he awoke the safe was open and the necklace gone.

She was adamant I had been in her arms all night. Luckily the bodyguard outside confirmed that I had not once left the room. Of course I hadn't, but I didn't need to protest my innocence. She was outraged on my behalf and would hear no word against me. I convinced her that the man must be suffering from shock and confusion following his ordeal, and thus stopped her from sacking him on the spot, but it was curious.

The police were called. The hotel searched. I lost count of the times that our room, the suite, myself and, on my insistence, my room was searched, but to no avail. The necklace had vanished as if it has never been there.

She needed my comfort for the rest of her stay. She even insisted on paying my hotel bill so that I would stay longer with her. Two days later when she was leaving she begged me to accompany her. I pleaded pressure of work and promised to join her in the Maldives a few days later when I had tied up a few loose ends in my own business.

I waved her and her entourage off and packed up my things. I spent the rest of the day in the Ashmolean then took a train to Paddington to meet my twin brother James. By now he will have fenced some of the stones from the necklace, He can have his share, I can repay my chum the two grand with interest, then sell the rest of the stones.- all except for the Blue Idol. I have to keep that for myself; It's just too beautiful and too hot to sell on.

Sometime after midnight that night, James, my identical twin had walked into the hotel dressed exactly like me. He passed the night porter on the desk jauntily wishing him "Goodnight" after a late night walk before turning in. Knowing that I like to keep fit, the night porter had thought nothing of it when James took the stairs up to our suite instead of the lift, only he hadn't. He had hidden for the next three hours in the stairwell until putting into operation our masterplan. It worked like a charm.

I love the feel of the stone in my hand, the colour, the clarity. I could just gaze at it for hours! It is mesmerizing - such beauty. No woman can match it, it captivates me.

A pity about the widow, she was rather nice; but I cannot join her in the Maldives. James and I will be on our way to Monte Carlo by then.

The Stairs

Julia crept under the back breakfast room window, narrowly missing cracking her head on the green slatted wooden shutter. To her right the terraced garden fell sharply away - a green slope peppered with daisies. To her left, the back door leading to the boot room and kitchen. She slipped in through the back door and crept down the hall. She could hear voices in the main front room. She felt resentful that these people should be here, in her house, without her permission. A rather hideous hat stand stood in the hall (her hall) where her long case clock should be. Julia came to the bottom of the stairs. She loved this staircase, it was the central piece of the house, dissecting the front room from the library and sweeping in a majestic fashion round to swirling balustrades each side. She started slowly ascending the staircase, the familiar feeling of dread beginning to grip her insides. Sure enough, as usual, she got halfway up the treads when a cold feeling gripped her and a misty figure could be dimly seen descending towards her. The feeling of hostility was tangible. The figure grew closer and closer to her. Just as Julia felt she would stop breathing altogether she awoke. It had been her recurring dream - the same one almost every night.

Julia and Steve were happy in their semi-detached house on the south coast. The one thing that would make Julia's life complete would be a move to the country, to the house of her dreams. The house that Julia dreamt of night after night was a detached double fronted Georgian pile. In her dreams it had green window shutters and a large overgrown terraced lawn. Steve had been doing well in his job and last month had been offered a promotion as an area manager. The only proviso was that they relocated to North Yorkshire. Julia saw it as an opportunity to find a house in the country and it was with great excitement that they drove to their bed and breakfast accommodation in the Yorkshire Dales for a week of house hunting and getting to know the area.

They looked at the properties they had chosen from their internet search. Some seemed to meet their needs but Julia viewed them all with lukewarm interest. Nothing seemed to grab her. She couldn't really see them living in any of them and Steve wasn't keen on any of them either. On day three they were driving through a small dales village. On the outskirts of the village she saw it. The house of her dreams! There it was on the hill, facing the road, with the large rambling gardens dropping away down the hill behind it.

Detached, surrounded by a picket fence and at least a quarter of a mile from the nearest neighbour. The window shutters with their peeling green paint stood open at either side of the heavy front door. Julia caught her breath and for a moment couldn't speak. Outside was a "for sale" sign! It was with an estate agent they had never heard of.

"We HAVE to have this house!" she told Steve, frantically punching the number of the agent into her phone. Steve doubted they could afford such a big place. He watched with some puzzlement as she ran around the sides of the fence looking across the view (familiar to her) at the back!

The agent was busy for the rest of that afternoon; he couldn't show them around until the following day. The owners of the house insisted on accompanied viewings since the lady of the house was of a 'nervous disposition'.

That night Julia did not dream of the house. She had very little sleep at all as she was so excited about it. Amazingly they could afford it. It was very cheap even allowing for the North/South difference in property prices. "We Just HAVE to have it!" she told herself over and over.

The following day they were so keen that they found themselves in the picturesque village with forty minutes to spare before their appointment with the estate agent. They went into the small coffee shop and ordered morning coffee. The owner wanted to chat. They told her of their mission to find a home and how Julia was set on Laurel Lodge. To their surprise she gave a wry smile: "It's cheap because Mrs Jowett wants out! She swears it's haunted!" Julia looked serious and leant forward: "How?" she asked breathlessly. "Well, I don't believe it myself." Continued their hostess. "I've dropped deliveries round to the kitchen and dining room many a time, and my friend, Mrs Arkwright, cleans for them and has never had any problem, but Mrs Jowett swears the main staircase is haunted! She reckons she sees a female form coming up the stairs! Personally I think it is the result of one sherry too many!"

The bell tinkled as a gentleman came through the door taking his cap off. "Morning George, the usual?" she enquired as she bustled back into the kitchen.

Julia became quiet, lost in thought, but Steve knew this would not put her off the house.

The agent showed them round the outside first, Julia knew her way already. As they paused to observe the view from the back Julia bent to retrieve a silver hoop earring from under the window to the right of the back door. She had the twin of this at home but had lost one so hadn't worn them for a while.

Once inside, Julia took charge, showing the agent and Steve around the downstairs as though she already lived there. As they climbed up the staircase Mrs Jowett came down to meet them. She gasped when she saw Julia and grabbed the bannister. She went so pale that the estate agent ran to the kitchen for water while Julia, sat her down on the stair.

"It's okay!" she told her, "Take some deep breaths." Then: "I found this earring in your garden. Have you lost one?" "I have never seen it before." said Mrs Jowett, "But I've seen YOU! You are my ghost! I see you at night coming up my stairs. Then you disappear!"

***

Three months later, Steve and Julia unlocked Laurel Lodge whilst awaiting the removal lorry. Mrs Jowett had moved into the nearby market town to be near her sister. She had been happier since the house went under offer and had not seen her ghost since.

Julia had never again had her repetitive dream. The silver earring, which she had slipped into her pocket that day on the stairs, matched her odd one at home exactly.

"We shall be happy here." she told Steve "Home at last!"

-Second Time Around

Tom watched her moving in the sunshine. Her young lithe body was so agile that it made him feel even older than he actually was. He could never keep up with her pace.

He hoped that she was happy here with him on the farm. It was a quiet life - just the two of them - he hoped it was enough for her. She was different to Beth. Beth and he had learnt and grown together. She had moved in with him just after he had inherited his father's farm, so they had had to learn things the hard way. They rubbed along really well together and were a wonderful team, making a success of the farm. Beth was content after a hard day's work to sit quietly by the fire with Tom. There was little need for words; they understood each other and, deep in love they sat in companionable silence.

When Beth sickened and died suddenly, Tom was in bits. He could think of no reason to get out of bed in the mornings and dragged himself around his duties with a heavy heart. He almost packed up and sold the farm, but his friends rallied round him - helping out wherever they could, and encouraging him to continue. He survived the lambing and then the harvest. Eventually his soul was healed enough for him to love the farm again.

He was still on his own. His friends tried to get him to go out with them. Occasionally he gave in and went to the pub for a pint or two, but, mostly, he preferred to stay home alone mourning the loss of Beth and staring into the fire for hours at a time.

His friend James had introduced them. He brought Sally over with him one evening. She was very young, but so beautiful. She had a way of looking at Tom that melted his heart and made his knees go weak. Her eyes were a peculiar hazel, almost orange, like a hare's eyes. She had a way of holding her head slightly to one side when Tom addressed her and her young body was so nimble and the way she moved was amazing.

She soon had him captivated and moved in with him a short time afterwards.. She showed him her love time and time again in a hundred different ways, but Tom had rubbed along so easily with Beth that it would take a deal of patience to get Sally trained in his ways and for him to trust her around the farm. She was a keen worker and seemed to be a quick learner. Tom just couldn't believe that one so young and beautiful with so much to offer could be happy with just him and the remote hillside farm.

One day it happened. Tom had driven them into the market town to do his banking. He had left Sally in the Land Rover while he slipped into the bank. He suddenly heard a screech of brakes and to his horror saw Sally crossing the road right into the path of a white pick-up truck. She had failed to see it. He Froze. Sally froze. The truck stopped millimetres away from her. Tom raced across the street and scooped Sally into his arms. She was shaken but unharmed. The truck driver jumped out and gave them both a large piece of her mind! Tom could see that she was upset because she had been shaken as much as he and Sally had. "Why don't you park up and let us buy you coffee. We are really sorry!" He said.

Charlotte, the driver of the pick-up, agreed. One coffee, stretched to two. Sally really liked her and Tom was taken with her wit, conversation and ready smile. Charlotte really liked Sally as well, so Tom invited her to the farm the following weekend to see the lambs.

That had been six months ago. Charlotte moved in with Tom and Sally last week. Sally loves having a mistress as well as a master and has become such a good sheepdog that

Tom is entering her for the sheepdog trials right after the wedding. Charlotte has agreed to marry him and is proving an asset around the farm too. Now, of an evening, Tom can sit in silence by the fire with his two favourite ladies, and Sally can roll over for her new mistress or her master to tickle her tummy.

Coffee time Killer

Inspector Fogden looked around the kitchen. Everything was neat and clean - in apple pie order - except for the body at the kitchen table. Colin Rook was sprawled, face down, across his newspaper. His glasses were skewed across the end of his nose and a large trough shaped depression in the back of his skull, which was slowly oozing blood and brain matter. The Inspector thought it had probably been made by an iron pipe or baseball bat. Penny Rook, the distraught wife, was sobbing in the sitting room with a WPC. The sound of the radio and dishwasher were the only noises in the kitchen. Inspector "Misty" Fogden signalled to his Sergeant to switch off the radio and then said quietly so as not to disturb the grieving widow:

"Pop down to the corner shop and get Mrs Linkthwaite to confirm Mrs Rook's visit this morning, and tell SOCO they can start in here now."

Colin Rook had been a local solicitor. Up until that morning he had worked for the Crown Prosecution Service and was known to be short tempered and incredibly close when it came to finances. Misty thought that it was possibly a revenge attack by one of his previously convicted criminals. He went through to the sitting room to speak with Penny.

"Now, Penny love," he asked gently, "tell me again what happened." He sent the WPC through to put the kettle on while Penny explained (between sobs): "I just popped down to Linkthwaite's to pay the newspaper bill and get some milk. We never lock the back door. When I got back the door was wide open and......" here she trailed off into fresh sobbing.

"Okay, love!" said Misty, gently patting her shoulder, "Your sister is on her way." Penny and her Sister, June, were very close and she brightened a little at this.

"Start at the beginning." Said Misty. "Take your time."

"Well," began Penny, "Saturday mornings we always have a late breakfast. Colin likes - liked - to read the papers and have a second cup of coffee, while I load the dishwasher and wipe down the worktops. This morning I needed more milk for his second coffee. He never got to drink it!" Fresh sobbing wracked her body.

"Okay love, that's all for now!" Said Misty.

June arrived and the sisters clung to each other for a few minutes then Penny asked June if she would stay with her as she didn't want to stay at June's. She was vaguely aware that she had all the financial, insurance and other matters to sort out, not to mention arranging the funeral. They would have to release Colin's body first, of course. She was thinking aloud to her sister but she sounded so likely to break down into hysterics again that June agreed at once.

Finally the police had finished and the body was taken away. After yet another cup of coffee, June went upstairs to make up the spare bed while Penny went into the kitchen to clear up after the police. It all looked much the same as ever, she slowly went over events in her mind while she unloaded the dishwasher and put things away.

Colin was mean - incredibly tight fisted and miserly - he had scolded her yesterday for ordering the charity Christmas cards. "Waste of money!" He had said. "Silly bits of paper for just a two day event."

This morning's row had been over June and the boys. Penny had wanted them all to come for Christmas. June was a widow and Penny enjoyed her company and that of her two teenage sons. Colin had refused. He shouldn't be expected to keep her family as well, he had told her. Did she think that her little pathetic part time job in the book shop would pay for them all eating him out of house and home? Anyway, by

Christmas she would have to be looking for somewhere else to live. He was leaving her and selling the house. They had no children, so he didn't have to pay her anything! Then he had dropped the bombshell that he and Valerie, his legal executive were setting up home together. He owed it to himself to have an intelligent partner, someone less boring and not such a spendthrift (and so on, in similar vein).

Penny relived all the hurtful humiliating things he had said as she unloaded the dishwasher. She took out the marble rolling pin. It was spotlessly clean now. It hadn't been when she had smashed it into the back of Colin's skull as he berated her! It had been such a relief though, when he had instantly shut up!

She had placed it carefully into the dishwasher with all of their previous night's clean crockery and put it on for another full cycle. Then, picking up her purse, she had quickly walked to the shop leaving the back door open behind her. On her return she had run, screaming, to the neighbours. It was they who had rung the police.

She would never be able to use that rolling pin again, she told herself, and the dishwasher would most probably have bits of bone and brain matter in the filter, even though she would try to clean and disinfect it once all the fuss had died down. She would probably take it to the local dump in any case, and she would buy a new dishwasher. She would also buy a new rolling pin! She could buy whatever she wanted now. A slow smile came over her face as she realised that June and the boys could come for Christmas after all. They could even move in if they wanted to. She could do whatever she felt like doing. She was free. It was all she could do not to skip into the sitting room singing. Instead she put the kettle on for yet another coffee!

The Old House

Jack burst through the door, wild-eyed and panting for breath. "Quick, Mattie, they are hot on my heels! Please tell me you haven't got a fire in."

"Not in the parlour, Jack, quick! Through here." She cried in reply.

Jacob Harvey - Jack to his friends - was a notorious scoundrel; a highwayman, fraudster and an incurable womaniser. Tonight he had almost fallen into an ambush set by the local constables. Riding back through the woods, he had abandoned his horse and run the last half mile to Mattie's house and potential safety.

Matilda Spriggs knew that she was just one of his many conquests, but he was a charmer; handsome and very generous with other people's purloined treasures. She was useful to him. Many a time she had hidden him when the law were pursuing him.

Mattie lived in one of the oldest houses in the village. It had a huge fireplace in the parlour. Since Mattie lived mainly in the kitchen, which was snug and had a range and oven, the parlour was only used on high days and holidays or when visitors were there.

Jack had installed extra bricks all the way up the chimney as hand and foot holds by which he could climb up onto the roof and make his escape once the coast was clear. As he climbed the bricks he thought that he really should wait until the men were gone, but the last time he had hidden here Mattie had been baking and the heat from the next chimney was so great he was half suffocated by the time she had called him down. It was a dark night. He would get out though the square chimney then slip away down the back cat-slide roof so that he could double back to the woods. He might even find his horse again and the constables would be miles away in the opposite direction.

Soot was clogging his throat and nostrils when he finally saw a thin watery half -moon through the opening above him. Climbing towards it with relief, he little thought that Constable Smeed would have stationed a man at the back of Mattie's house. Constable Grey looked up just as Jack's head and shoulders emerged from the chimney stack. Taking aim with his flintlock pistol he fired. A lucky shot! It caught Jack square in the forehead. Without uttering a sound he fell back down the chimney and landed in an undignified heap on the hearth at a wailing Mattie's feet!

.****

Some 190 years later Petra and David were house hunting. They were viewing the old house and Petra instantly felt drawn to the wide inglenook fireplace in the lounge.

"We have to have this house!" she whispered to David, even though they still hadn't explored the upstairs and it was priced a little higher than they had wanted.

David liked the house, the location was ideal for their work, and it did have character, he had to admit. Petra was so excited she could hardly contain herself. She made all sorts of plans for the rooms and garden.

"We can put a wood-burner in the big fireplace." said David, "It will be much more economical." "NO WAY!" Petra almost shouted, "Leave that fireplace alone! It is perfect as it is."

She seemed so worked up about it that David thought it wisest to leave well alone. On every other aspect they agreed perfectly.

They moved in and quickly settled. For the first few weeks life was uneventful and they were blissfully happy.

One evening after work, Petra decided she would light a fire in the lounge. The nights were drawing in and she felt a little chilly. David wasn't due home for another half an hour and she thought a nice blazing fire would cheer him.

Leaning into the fireplace, she suddenly felt a strange feeling of familiarity - something imperceptible and not entirely pleasant. Inexplicably she felt a great sorrow, almost like a bereavement. Lighting the fire she went into the kitchen and poured herself a large glass of red wine. It was some time before she could shake off the feeling. David loved the fire and they spent a cosy evening in front of it before bed.

Petra was cleaning the ashes out one morning a few days later, when David sneaked up behind her and threw his arms around her. Smiling she turned and, instead of David's face, she saw a strange man. He was a little shorter than David, with shoulder length brown hair, a pointed beard and very piercing grey eyes. He was handsome and looked familiar, but, nonetheless, she screamed with shock. This dispelled the image and David stood in front of her, his arms around her waist. He calmed her and apologised for scaring her. She laughed it off but felt shaken by it all the same.

Autumn wore on and turned to winter. Petra longed to get home to her fireplace and get the logs burning. One evening she walked into the house and felt for the light switch. To her consternation she couldn't find it. The house seemed barer in the dark and she fumbled her way into the lounge where she knew candles and matches were kept in the cupboard. Lighting a candle she looked around. The room was different. The air was heavy and everything felt still and oppressive. As if in a trance Petra lit candle after candle and placed them in a semi-circle around the fireplace. Sitting on the hearth, she closed her eyes. She could feel him near her, the man with the grey eyes and long hair. She felt his arms encircle her and laid her head back onto his shoulder. Just then the room was illuminated with electric light!

"What the devil are you doing sitting all alone in the dark here?" asked a puzzled David.

Petra noticed the room was back to its old familiar self, but she offered David no explanation.

Winter wore on. Petra would often rush home to sit in the dark, by candlelight, in the old fireplace until David came home. Sometimes, when he kissed her, or when they were alone together in bed, Petra would look up and see the face of the bearded man with long hair looking at her, his grey eyes twinkling with amusement.

One evening Petra raced home and lit the candles. In the dark he came to her. Enfolding her in his arms they lay on the hearth together. That is where David found her on his return from work, cold, and quite dead with a rapturous look on her face.

*****

Four months later David had moved away and the estate agent was showing another couple around the old house. The man was somewhat reserved but the young woman became very animated when they viewed the lounge.

"We have to have this house!" she told her partner, "I LOVE that fireplace...."

Vengeance

Isaac Davies listened to the long-case clock resolutely ticking the minutes and hours away. The bar downstairs had gone quiet now and Jeremiah (Jem) was driving him mad flicking the lid of his snuff box open and closed repeatedly, with a maddening click-snap click-snap. Isaac was at the window of the upstairs room of the inn. "Where the bloody hell is that signal?" he snapped, irritably.

The men were members of a successful gang of free traders (or smugglers, as we would know them today). The Bridport gang operated from the small seaports off the Dorset and Somerset coast. The Ring o' Bells Inn, commonly known as the Bells, was their regular meeting place and the upstairs room their hideout. They could signal to the small fishing boats out at sea from the window and also see the signal for the all clear, when they could come down to unload and secrete the cargo away in various hiding places. Henry Burgess was the landlord and a prominent member of the gang.

Tonight the signal was late. The weather had been bad so the landing was delayed; but now it should be clear for the little boat from Cherbourg, or perhaps Roscoff, to land the contraband on the secluded beach.

Henry was on the beach with the tubsmen to cut free and carry the cargo, and a few batsmen to protect them while they unloaded. They would signal the boat if it was safe to land, then signal again to the men at the inn once it had landed. They in turn would return the signal if it was safe to bring it from the beach up the steep cobbled village street to the various 'safe houses'.

The clock ticked. Jem clicked and snapped at the snuff box. Isaac still felt irritated. Suddenly a muffled scream sounded from downstairs. Isaac and Jem froze, looking at each other in horror. Before either could rise up men's voices and heavy footsteps were heard running up the stairs. The door burst open to reveal Lieutenant Harding, the excise man, with half a dozen burly dragoons, their flintlock pistols levelled. Having been shackled, each to a dragoon they were led downstairs past Henry's sobbing wife - herself held firmly by another soldier - to an awaiting prison carriage. Inside were a heavily ironed Henry and the others. They set off for the long drive to Dorchester gaol.

Their trial came up at the next Dorchester Assize. It was a mystery to Isaac and the others how they had been found out. The gang's activities had gone on undisturbed for the past six years, it almost seemed, as if the costal blockade force had turned a blind eye to their nefarious doings. They weren't hurting anyone, and apart from the odd skirmish involving beatings on both sides, no one had been killed. True, the authorities had levied a £300 reward to anyone bringing news resulting in the capture of the gang, but people in fairly high places bought the illicit goods. Most of the locals benefitted one way or another from the gangs' work, therefore, no one was inclined to expose them. Then, on day two of the trial, to the surprise of the gang, two vital witnesses were called by the prosecuting counsel.

Charles Spink and Paul Sweeney had previously been prominent members of the gang. They had proved problematic though as Paul was an inveterate drunkard, liable to let his mouth run away with him when in his cups. He would often tap the very tubs on his back and boasted to anyone who would listen of his unlawful exploits. Henry and Isaac feared it would expose the gang. Charles was getting older. He couldn't carry tubs, keep up with the others, or handle the big oak cudgels used to protect them anymore. Henry still paid him to store some of the contraband in his outhouse, but he held a grudge as he resented this demotion from the gang's activities.

Despite the valiant efforts of their defence counsel, the trial went badly for them. Henry, Isaac and Jem were sentenced to hang the following Monday. The rest of the gang, ten of the tubmen and batsmen were sentenced to transportation for life to Van Diemen's land. As they were taken down to the cells, Henry and Isaac swore revenge on Sweeney and Spink, and cursed them for eternity! There was much sorrow and hardship in the village following the demise of the gang. Forty children were left fatherless by the executions and transportations and the parish had to raise the money to reunite loved ones with their husbands and fathers in Australia in later years. Sweeney and Spink were the only ones who prospered thanks to their ill- gotten gains!

*****

The Bells was buzzing; a party was in full swing. This was the year 2018, some two hundred years after the smuggling gang were caught. Two visitors to the village were being honoured with a party in the pub. James Mattocks and Paul Hayes, descendants of some of the transported batsmen, were over from the Antipodes to visit their English cousins, the Burgesses.

Whilst they had written regularly and spoken on *Skype*, this was their first visit to the mother country. Indeed, at one time the Burgesses had run the Bells; Henry's widow and children struggling to keep it going for some years after his execution, eventually selling it to Isaac's descendants, the Davies, who ran it to this day.

Many of the gang's descendants had come to the party to welcome the visitors as the Bells thrived on its reputation as 'the Smuggler's pub and headquarters of the Bridport Gang.'

Now the local magistrate and lay preacher was a certain Reginald Spink, he and the local MP Brian Sweeney had also been invited whilst the local paper had sent their reporter, Nick Gorringe, descendant of the ill- fated Jem, to report on the 'Reunion of the Bridport Gang' from both Australia and England!

Drink flowed, chatter and laughter filled the pub and Nick took copious notes. Many photos were taken of the evening. Occasionally the odd wink or whispered aside would come from the Australian visitors to Nick or their cousins and the landlady slipped upstairs to make a phone call, but everyone was having a good time. Eventually it was time to close the celebrations for the evening. A final toast was proposed and everyone drained their glasses and started to drift off to their homes or cars.

As Brian Sweeney drove off he was flagged down two hundred yards from the pub by a police check patrol - called earlier by the landlady. He confidently agreed to take their breathalyser test as he had drunk only orange juice (liberally laced with several double vodkas, unbeknown to him.)

While he tried to protest this as a mistake, a second police patrol had pulled Reginald Spink over for a bald tyre (surreptitiously swapped for his usual one by George Burgess, the owner of the local garage). On examining the car they found a suspicious package of white powder in the glovebox, this would later prove to be cocaine.

How fortunate that Nick Gorringe was there. Not only would their downfall be a good read in the local paper, but thanks to Brian Sweeney's position, he knew he had scooped a national story too; good for business for the Bells as well and something for the highly amused Antipodean crew to tell their grandchildren!

Martha of the Dell

It was quiet here, grey and damp, overshadowed by the stark trees and damp mulch of orangey brown leaves under foot. The air here smelt of a mixture of decay and charred wood, a vague bonfire smell still lingering.

Tara had set out across the fields from her home after the phone call, her eyes blurred with tears. She had no idea where she was going, so was surprised to find that she had walked as far as the dell behind St Georges' churchyard. It was always a bit gloomy there, a heavy sadness in the air. It matched her mood perfectly. Tom! Oh how could he! She had thought him the love of her life. She had been convinced that he felt the same way. He had told her so. They were going to set up home together.

Lately she had thought he might be seeing someone else - a 'bit on the side'. The texts that he answered then deleted, telling her it was just work; the late nights when he couldn't see her - 'out with the boys' or 'meeting clients'. He soothed her, pleaded that he was just busy - he loved her didn't he? So she buried her head in the sand and continued with her plans and her dreams.

Last night he stood her up and his phone was turned off. After a morning of tears he had finally rung her an hour ago. He had been seeing someone else. He explained that the other woman was pregnant and so he would have to finish with Tara and 'do the right thing'.

"How could you get your bit on the side pregnant and ruin your proper relationship with me?" She had wailed at him

Then he had hit her like an express train and, with as much devastation. He told her that she, Tara, was the 'bit on the side' and he had got his long term partner, whom he had been living with for the past two years, pregnant; so now he had to shoulder his responsibilities!

She had dropped the phone, flung herself on her bed and sobbed. Then, with a vague idea in her head, she had grabbed the spare clothesline from under the sink and headed to the dell across the fields where she knew there were some sturdy trees. She felt such despair. Life held no joy or future for her at that moment. She came across a huge ancient, sturdy oak and leant her forehead against its trunk sobbing. She failed to notice the small lady dressed in very old fashioned clothing. The sort of thing housemaids wore in early Victorian times. This small lady stepped out from behind the tree and stood next to Tara, her face hidden behind the lower branches.

"Nothing is worth that, m'dear." She said, as if reading Tara's mind, then, "Is it a man? Huh! Yes, it usually is. Believe me time heals, there is a future."

Tara was amazed that this young lady - for her voice gave her age away - could be so perceptive as to feel her pain. She found herself telling this odd stranger all about Tom and his treachery. As she spoke, she already felt lighter. The strange girl kept her face hidden but said to Tara: "His pregnant lady is the real victim here. You have had a lucky escape m'dear. She is stuck with a false ne'er do well. He will never be faithful to her. Forget him and embrace life whilst you can. Believe me he is not worth it. I know!" With that Tara looked up and the lady was gone.

Drying her tears, Tara felt calmer now. She walked through the dell and through the gate to the churchyard, intending to go and sit in the church to think. When she got there, St George's was full of noise and colour. She discovered that it was celebrating its eight hundred and fiftieth anniversary with a pageant. Villagers had dressed in period costume dating from the middle ages to the present day. Tara bought a church guide book from a Norman peasant on the door.

Tea and cakes were being sold in the Lady Chapel. Buying herself a cup of tea from a diminutive lady dressed as a Victorian housemaid, she whispered: "Thank you for your advice in the dell." She then settled down on a vacant pew to read her guidebook.

She read the history of the church and the close links it had with the local squire and his family. She read of the sad story of Martha, a Victorian housemaid who had fallen pregnant by the squire's son. When he had refused to acknowledge her or the child, she had gone to the dell, found the biggest, oldest oak tree and had hung herself from its sturdy branches. According to the guide book her restless spirit is said to haunt the dell to this day.

Repressing a shudder, Tara felt sad, not for herself or the loss of Tom, but for poor Martha, who had had no one to turn to in her darkest hour. The lady serving tea must be dressed as her, she thought to herself. She seemed a little older than Martha though; no wonder she had hidden her face when they met in the dell.

Over in the Lady Chapel and by the tea urns, the tea lady's husband asked her: "What did that girl mean, your advice in the dell?" "I really have no idea whatsoever!" Said the tea lady, "You know full well, we have been so busy we haven't left here all afternoon!"

In the dell a shadow merged with the damp leaves as the dusk began to gather.

The Glorious Few

Roddy flew onwards across a sky beginning to turn crimson with the dying rays of the day's sun. He could see dear old Blighty spread out beneath him, the chequered fields and hedges and here and there the point of a church spire breaking up the flat appearance of the villages below.

He wondered at the difference in the buildings as he flew over the countryside, from the plain windowed Norman towered stone churches of East Anglia to the great stately Cathedrals of some of the English cities. Roddy felt a great sense of relief at the sight of the English countryside below them, especially as they drew near to his beloved Kent. He had wanted this for as long as he could remember. He loved flying and had always wanted to lead, like his father before him. When he was offered his own squadron, it seemed like the greatest thing imaginable, but along with the glory came the responsibility - the fact that all those other lives depended on him, his orders and his decisions. They really could mean the difference between life and death, and not just his own.

He had a major scare when Bernie had nearly bought it over Normandy, and to add to the fright, it had been ground fire that had damaged the wing and nearly sent him whirling in an uncontrollable spin to crash onto the earth below. Luckily he had managed to limp down safely and, once they had all got over the scare, they assessed the damage. It was only a scratch from the bullets, it would be repaired in a few days, but Roddy had had to leave two of his companions with Bernie to escort him home from behind enemy lines. Safety in numbers; that had been dinned into him from both his father and his instructors at flying school. So now a much depleted flight was limping home to dear old England for a well-earned rest; headed towards comfort, good food and, above all, safety.

For some of the younger ones this had been their first trip to foreign climes. They were, none of them, very old and, looking back, they had still been wet behind the ears; a really naïve bunch of idealistic innocents, starry eyed and full of dreams of glory and heroism; but the reality was that the world was full of many dangers. They would not all come back. To Roddy's grief they had already lost two of their number. With Bernie and his two escorts that only left three quarters of the original number that had started the long flight. Whilst he was still very young himself, he hoped he had been a good commander and certainly took his role very seriously, placing the safety of them all above everything else.

Roddy looked down at the landscape below, he always felt the thrill of excitement when he drew near to the beloved sanctuary he had always considered as home. Below them spread the marshes of Romney in Kent. He could see all the ancient small churches - some medieval, some ruined - that dotted the landscape. There were sheep (lots and lots of sheep) but, more importantly, he knew that they would be greeted with security, and comfort. They would sing the old songs and have fun with every need catered for in a place of safety, where they could have a well-earned rest and recuperate for a few weeks. His heart flipped with joy as he spotted the familiar landmarks below, there was the little steam train, chugging across the landscape, the old black lighthouse with the white top and the sprawling power-station blighting the landscape, but somehow reassuring none the less. He gave the order to descend and the familiar tension crept over him. Landing could be the most tricky part of the mission.

They had made it; home safe and sound under his command. He breathed a sigh of relief and they all cheered. Only then did they spy their old friends coming to meet them, to welcome them back for the season. They were reassured that Bernie's flight would be with them before the week was out and Roddy was congratulated on a successful first mission. He had safely brought his squadron of Canada geese back to the Dungeness Nature reserve from their winter migration in Norway.

Life's a gamble

I watched him walking towards the bridge. His pain was palpable, and determination was written all over his face. I just knew what he was thinking. I hoped against hope that I was wrong; but, even as I hoped, I saw him climbing over the railings. I called out to him even though I knew he couldn't possibly hear me. I hoped she would be in time.

Where was she? I had sent her especially and she wasn't here yet. I could see him standing on the wrong side of the railings looking down from the bridge to the river, tears coursed down his face unchecked. I doubted he was even aware of them. His eyes had that distant distracted look I knew so well. I had seen that look hundreds of times before.

Even from my viewpoint I could see his determined stance and the expression adopted prior to a leap. Where was she? Had she gone back on the deal? Then there she was, at last.

We both saw her - a child of about six or seven years - her golden curls blowing in the breeze as the boat sailed down the river. She was holding her teddy and trailing her hand in the water. Then the child dropped her teddy into the water from the pleasure cruiser and leant too far over the side to retrieve it. I smiled to myself as I saw the horror on his face and his mouth wide open in a silent scream as she plopped into the water unnoticed by her father, at the helm with the radio blaring.

For someone in so much despair, he moved very quickly. Taking the metal steps to the riverbank two at a time he virtually threw himself down screaming to her father to stop the boat, whilst flinging off his jacket and kicking off his shoes. Grabbing a lifebuoy ring, he jumped in and swam towards the little girl as she sank down for the second time.

He threw the ring over her as she surfaced and held her while her father pushed the boathook towards them, his face white as a sheet and registering total shock and panic.

I knew she would be fine. It was part of the deal, it wasn't her time yet. This would help them both.

I had seen her face when she sank for the second time. She had looked terrified but her eyes met mine knowingly. I could have sworn that there was gratitude in them, even amidst the terror.

I saw them both safely helped into the boat by her father while onlookers called for an ambulance. Blankets were wrapped around them. For the first time in ages, the man looked interested in his surroundings and, yes, perhaps even in life itself.

They insisted he be taken to hospital for a check over. The child's father was crying with relief and gratitude, hugging his daughter to him while praising the man's quick action and bravery. Everything had changed in an instant. From the depths of feeling such dark despair, he had been forced to feel concern; to care so much that he didn't stop to think about anything other than saving this child. The man was grateful for the instant transformation in his life. He was also grateful that this child had been saved - unlike his own child.

He hadn't been able to save her - nothing could once the illness had reached its final stage. Rescuing this little girl had helped a little. It had eased the feeling of total impotence, illogical guilt, and pointlessness that he had been feeling ever since he lost her.

Deep in her soul, the child knew that the action of putting herself in peril had saved her soul and had gone some way towards atoning for the sins she had committed in a previous life. They both looked shaken, but hope also gleamed from both their eyes.

I felt relief. This time it had been fair, as agreed when I won. The reaper had not gone back on the deal, as he has been known to do in the past.

Guardian angels, like me, have a hard time of it. We have to play and barter for people's souls. Last night I had beaten the reaper soundly at chess. The two souls just preserved had been mine, won fair and square in last night's game. They would live, and yes, they would go on to do much good in this world (Heaven knows we need it).

I turned away from the river scene and flew back upstairs. I had a big game of poker tonight, playing Lucifer himself for the souls of a regiment of soldiers. I needed to rest first as this was to be a hard match and who could say how it would end? I may win but devils are not to be trusted. It is a matter of life or death and it's all a gamble!

Part two

The next two stories are offered with humble apologies to C. S. Lewis, who very probably is not actually spinning in his grave very much!

The Grufferty Letters

(Discovered, quite by chance, by Lyn Watts on a laptop in a kennel somewhere in darkest Sussex)

These are a series of instructional letters to my dog, Tyson, which I found when I discovered his secret I-Pad whilst de-fleaing his bed. I managed to crack the password (which was easy as he always uses 'Sausages'.) They are letters, (or, more precisely, e-mails - since dogs can't write; not having an opposable thumb) from his wise old Uncle Grufferty, long deceased from this life and now living over the rainbow bridge. They go a long way to explaining some of Tyson's behaviour so I thought I should publish them so that every dog owner can be enlightened.

My dear nephew Tyson,

I have been chosen by the Keeper of the Bridge, to be your spiritual guide and mentor while you spend your time on Earth. Humans can be tricky things to handle and it is vital that we dogs learn the art of manipulation early, in order to control them. There is nothing worse than a two legged friend who has been allowed to become out of control. This is anti-social and will win you no friends in the canine world! Should this happen, they will then try to rule you. Clearly this is against the order of things and must NOT be allowed under ANY circumstance. It is, therefore, my duty to educate you in such matters of etiquette and manners expected in the dog/human relationship. We will start with the **Matter of Mealtimes.**

I was horrified to see that, due to your inexperience, the two legged ones were able to eat a whole roast dinner, feeling guiltless and without giving you even an undercooked potato. This really lets the side down and displeases the Bridge keeper greatly. You must learn. When ANY human food is around it is our DUTY to make them feel so guilty that, unless they share it with us, it is as sawdust in their mouths. The first thing to try is to sit really close, looking as soulful and sad as you can. Really work those big doleful eyes; if that alone isn't enough try forcing some drool and dribble out of the sides of your mouth and suck your gut in to look thin and hungry. This drooling is a bit of a risk as they may be disgusted and banish you to your bed, In which case default to 'sulk mode' (to be addressed later), but, if this is not the case, the next stage is the 'paw treatment'. Raise a front paw stiffly to human knee height then let it subtly slide down the side of the leg making sure that the claws scrape painfully at the skin, repeat until you get a result, all the while drooling and wagging your backside from side to side allowing the tail to brush the carpet as you do. It helps if you can emit the odd whimper or two as well. Should they be the hardened two legged type and this still yields no result then we try the 'freak them out' tactic. Pretend to suddenly lose interest and gaze at an imaginary ghost either on the ceiling or in the corner of the room. Keep your gaze fixed and ears pert. Don't waver and ignore them if they speak to you, so intently are you watching the ghost of their Great Uncle Horace, or whomever their consciences fear may be haunting them. This often results in them being so freaked out that, having failed to distract you with voice command, they will shake a piece of roast beef or the odd potato at you to make it stop.

If this has still not brought about the desired effect, things call for desperate measures; after all, the dinner must be nearly eaten by now. Suddenly stiffen the back, erect the ears and bark like crazy running to the front door and back whining occasionally between frantic hysterical barks. They will think that there is an unexpected caller at the door and then, when they leave the table to investigate, you can seize your chance and blatantly steal the damn dinner! It will be worth them yelling and berating you, you can then use that as an excuse for a long guilt-making sulk under the table. This can be really effective at times, but the art of sulking will come at a later date my lad, once you have mastered manipulation.

Good luck with it, your affectionate Uncle
Grufferty

My dear nephew Tyson,

On the subject of **Travel**

My spies below tell me that you are about to be taken on a long car journey by your two legged guardians. This offers endless possibilities for amusement and you will be fully expected by the Bridge Keeper to uphold these duties. Firstly it is essential that you make their journey as miserable as caninely possible. Not with any prior warning you understand. Oh No ! If they got wind of this they may slip a Mickey into your Barkers incomplete or Chumalot, then you would sleep most of the way and miss a golden opportunity. Wait until about three miles from home and start with a gentle whimper and the occasional yelp. After about fifteen minutes of this increase to a frantic yelping and whining. They won't stand too much of this before the female one will convince the other one that you need to 'spend a penny'. Stupid humans; dogs don't need money, they get everything for free! However, this usually results in them stopping the car and putting your lead on before (optimistically) taking you to the nearest tree. At this point it is CRUCIAL that you act normally, sniff and mess around for ages, be sure to eat plenty of grass (this is essential for later) but do NOT - I repeat NOT - actually pee, (or anything else). Once this proves fruitless they will offer you a drink of water. It is expected that you sniff with distain and then completely ignore it. They will put you back into your safe place behind the dog guard or in crate and continue the journey. The next part is imperative to the success of this mission so listen carefully.

Once they are on the fastest moving motorway, preferably with at least forty five miles to the nearest services, whine hysterically, interspersed with frantic ear splitting yelps and barks, then start loudly retching and coughing! They will be getting extremely stressed as there will be nowhere for them to pull over safely at this point. Once the elastic of their nerves is at snapping point, vomit in the most loud, revolting and gut turning way you possibly can. This will be aided by your ingestion of grass earlier. For extra bonus points, and maximum nauseous making effect, eat as much rubbish as you can find in the garden before the journey! They will then have to travel with this for at least the next forty miles or so, thus guaranteeing that you need not travel too often on long, boring journeys, in the back of the car. This will, of course, risk having your name changed to "Shutupandliedowndamnyou" but it will be worth it!

Wishing you every good luck with it all

Your affectionate Uncle

Grufferty.

My dear Nephew Tyson,

Walks, the importance of smelly substances and how to sulk!

One endearing thing the two legged ones do (or should do) is to take you out for 'walkies' two or three times a day. These are usually a good interesting way of reading the local news by way of your nose, and having a game or two with a stick, ball or a 'wanger' depending on the fitness level and enlightenment of your human. It is obligatory for you to whine with excitement at the first rattle of the lead and jump about, generally getting under the feet of the two legged one and, for extra bonus points, head butting them on the nose as you jump up at the exact moment they bend to attach your lead. Sometimes these walks can be a real chore, especially if it is raining, windy, or just too hot outside. However, this is irrelevant. Drag yourself up and still make a pretence of being mad keen as they will probably hate the adverse elements even more than you do, (remember they have to be out in it too). One thing to look for on these walks is something really smelly to roll in. If it happens to be sticky too that will get you maximum bonus points, especially if you have a long furry coat for it to adhere to. There are many nasty substances, chewing gum causes maximum removal effort but doesn't quite have the 'yeuk' factor that , say, fox poo does. Good old fox poo! We HAVE to roll in any we find; it is in the contract! The problem is that the human will be aware of this and try to distract you. Play along with it, let them think you have forgotten about the demonic steaming pile, play with the wanger ball, chase their silly stick, even retrieve it if you MUST, but lull them into a sense of false security. Once they have forgotten the poo, sneak back and have a good old hundred and eighty degree roll all over it, really rub it in, then fix a ridiculous grin on your face and bound affectionately up to them for some petting. Rub yourself round their legs like a cat, wagging your tail to join in the excitement that your current state has no doubt produced in them. This stuff has a double bonus of being really smelly (but also really difficult to remove, or at least the smell is!) The smell could linger around for weeks. The down side is, of course, that this will earn you a new Russian sounding nickname of 'Tysonbuggeroff' and will undoubtedly result in the dreaded bath time. In vain will you shove your head under the sofa, in vain will you stiffly push all four legs against the door frame, into the tub you will go! Nil

Desperandum, my dear chap – endless possibilities for fun. Wait until you are soaked and bedraggled in the tub then:

1) Pretend to be so afraid that you pee yourself (or worse for extra points)

2) shake yourself so hard that the human, the walls, the surrounding fitments and the floor get soaked and spotted with poo coloured water.

3) Shake again when out of the tub before they can dry you, then sulk under the table for hours. You can always sneak into the kitchen and eat your supper without them noticing if you get back under the table quickly enough.

The success of this whole mission depends on your ability to remember where you saw the reserve pile of fox poo, so that on your next walk, when they purposely avoid the one you rolled in yesterday, you can innocently wander off to the reserve pile and do the whole fun thing all over again! We dogs have an overdeveloped thick skin so do not quail at the regrettable language used or the names called to you by your human. You will have earned your Chinese nickname of 'Fox Poo King'. You can always put into action the sulk routine! Sulking is useful for so many things, it eventually results in the human feeling like a bully, and trying to make up to you with extra treats etc. It can be used if you fail to get the mealtime treat at human's dinnertime, if you fail to evict the human from their chair, or if you are thrown off their bed. You can use it to get an extra walk, or to register your displeasure following a telling off or bath. Firstly make your eyes as sad as possible. Imagine that you are starving to death and are forced to watch as all around you are feasting; this will make your expression so pitiful that they will instantly start to feel bad. Slink under the nearest table with your ears down and tail tucked as far under your legs as is caninely possible. If you can, keep your back to them and totally ignore anything, I repeat ANYTHING, they may say, Including "here you are boy!" and "come on now, walkies!" They are trying to tempt you out. Do not have any of it. Let them suffer. The amount of time this goes on for can be in direct proportion to their offence, but can sometimes be as long as fifteen human minutes for the really serious offences. Only come out when something really worthwhile is offered and you are sure that the humans have learnt their lesson. The normal reaction following this is to give you your own way for several hours after a sulking bout.

Good Luck with it al

Your affectionate Uncle

Grufferty

My Dear Nephew Tyson

The matter of sleeping arrangements

Now the law of nature says we should sleep in packs. This is for warmth and protection, the idea being that there is safety in numbers to ward off the evil predators of the night time.

Our poor misguided humans may well have other ideas and expect you to sleep elsewhere, often downstairs. This is most unreasonable. How can they expect you to scare off the scavenging hyenas and wolves if you are in another part of the house. They may even have bought you some sort of ghastly contraption from the local Pet Mart called a dogbed! This will have, no doubt, cost them a small fortune by the time they have bought the matching sheepskin mattress and blankets. This MUST be avoided at all costs! Do NOT go near it. Yes, it may look comfortable, that cute fluffy squirrel (the one that squeaks) looks great fun to snuggle to and play with but have no truck with it whatsoever.

If they think that you like your bed, the masterplan is doomed to failure. They will settle you down on the first night, having let you out for a final trip in the garden. Up the stairs to bed they will go having shut you in the cosy warm kitchen on your cosy, warm, hated dogbed. Wait for a suitable length of time, just long enough for them to get comfortable and turn out the light , then put the master plan into action.

Start off at first with a gentle whimper. Try this three or four times, gradually rising the pitch and urgency. If this fails to get a reaction sit up and raise your nose to the ceiling, head back and let out a good old howl! This can also increase in pitch and volume until you are rivalling old Hellhound Cerebos himself, and the rafters are ringing with your cacophony! They will come down at first and try to settle you again. Have no part of it, repeat steps one and two. Their next tactic may be to let you out into the garden again 'just to be on the safe side'. Stand by the back doorstep looking wretched and refuse to move.

Keep this up for as long as needed being extra sure to wag your tail delightedly and grin every time they come downstairs (even though they are shouting at you and the language is truly, delightfully, shocking). They will eventually (about 2am, by my reckoning) realise that the only way to get any sleep is to bring you upstairs with them! Of course you are tired too, but you can snooze all day in the armchair while they are out and about working or shopping etc.

At first they will bring the hated dogbed contraption up with them and place it beside their bed for you to sleep in. Ignore it and get onto their bed the minute they open the bedroom door. They will, of course, scoop you off a few times depositing you in the dogbed and reinforcing their pathetic will with a firm "NO". If their will is harder to crack than you first thought then, eventually, you may have to appear to comply with their hated wishes and get in the dogbed. This need only be an emergency temporary measure because as soon as you hear them snoring, get up on their bed and snuggle.

You may well meet with some early resistance, but once they realise the benefit of your warm snuggly body next to theirs in the night you can put plan B into action. Get up onto the bed and turn around three times. No one knows why we do this, but it's in the contract! You need to convince them that you are there to protect them from predators. This should be easy. When was the last time anyone saw hyenas or bears in Surbiton, thus proving how efficient you are! Now gradually spread yourself out until you have the warm centre of the bed and they are given the very generous four inch edge at each side of the bed to balance on in their sleepy state for the rest of the night. If there are two of you this can apply to both top and bottom of the bed too! After all, in Greenland, the natives always use dogs for warmth so your humans will soon learn to appreciate the benefits of a two dog night!

Now the most effective alarm clock known to mankind is the sound of dog retching! The human who invents a mechanical clock with this sound for an alarm, will make millions! Midweek, they will no doubt have an annoying ringing sound that gets them out of bed really early (before light in some cases.) Hang on in there and only reluctantly get up when it looks as though you may miss out on breakfast.

Weekends are a different matter. This is when you must employ the retch technique. They want to lie in bed far too long on a nice sunny Saturday or Sunday. Dawn has broken, there are birds in the garden to chase and walks to be had with sticks to crunch and trees to…. well never mind; there is also breakfast to be had. They just want to sleep in late. When you want them to get up, start off with a loud swallowing and licking sound, increasing in pitch and speed. Then start the retching noise in your throat. Gag and make sure your body is wracked with spasms of muscle jerks and stand up on the bed. Within seconds one of them will push you to the floor. Make sure you hover over their best bedside rug or better still his slippers and retch and jerk the back and tummy muscles. If you can manage a little spasm of the throat and a gagging sound too without actually vomiting (succeeding might make them banish you from the room for ever) They will be quick to respond. Leaping from the bed they will have you downstairs and into the garden like greased lightning. Once there quickly eat some grass to enable you to bring up some frothy disgusting saliva like substance rendering them incapable of going back to bed thus bringing walk time nearer.

There is always the risk that they may not give you breakfast but you can very soon brighten up and employ the same tactics you have been taught to utilise at mealtimes until they crack under the pressure and strain.

Let me know how you get on
Your Affectionate Uncle
Grufferty.

My Dear Nephew Tyson

The sport of – Postman Baiting

It is a law known only unto themselves why, almost every day, the humans will receive small flat paper envelopes and leaflets through the slot in their front doors called the letterbox! Mostly these are received with groans and expressions like: "Not more junk - stick it in the recycling bin" or "Oh God! Not another b*****d (words too rude to repeat here) bill! Stick it behind the clock on the mantle with all the others" and other such utterances.

The vandal responsible for delivering this rubbish to the humans house is called a postman (or woman) affectionately known as 'the postie'! Now these characters sneak up the path and plop the pile of uninvited correspondence through said letterbox, then beetle back down the path again without so much as a by-your-leave. It is our job to terrorise them! To make their lives a misery!

No, you don't really have to sink your teeth into them. This will result in very serious consequences and may mean you join me here over the bridge somewhat prematurely. No, this is more about psychological warfare. Lay in wait by the front door but out of sight from the postie.

You will soon learn roughly the time of day they deliver to your house, wait until you see the postie's shadow through the glass panel then jump up, barking loudly and hysterically! If you can jump high enough to bark in his face through the glass panel you get extra bonus points. This should result in a gasp from said postie clutching at his chest the while, and a strong possibility of some rude words escaping his lips.

Once postie gets used to this you will lose the element of surprise. This calls for a change in tactics. Keep quiet and out of sight until the letterbox opens, then jump up, snatching the letters out of postie's hand and giving muffled growls and barks at the same time. This will cause alarm and despondency amongst the post office representatives coming to your house. Vary this somewhat and change the timings of your attack so that sometimes you jump up when postie arrives at the door, others when he turns to leave. Give no quarter, how dare he enter your domain with his silly bits of paper.

Should you be unfortunate enough to be outside when he calls and to come face to face with him, a change of tactics is called for. Wag the tail and bow down with an ingratiating grin and a submissive tilt to the head. Allow postie to pat and fuss you. Be as amiable and loving as a lapdog. This will be all the more effective the next time he calls and you are on your side of the door. Having been lulled into a false sense of security, he will be unprepared for the cacophony of barks and the snatching of the letters and the shock will be even greater. For maximum effect throw your body against the door until it shakes. The look on his face will be well worth the tiring effort. You must tell me how you get on.

Your affectionate Uncle

Grufferty.

My Dear Nephew Tyson,

Children and their toys

I know that you live in a childfree family, well for the most part at least. However, once every seven days or so the house will be invaded by mini human terrorists called grandchildren! Mostly the visit is just for the day but sometimes they will stay overnight for what the humans call 'the weekend'. We dogs, in common with the upper echelons of human society, don't have weekends. This is because we don't have working weeks. One day is much the same as another to us idle rich!

Now I know this is very disruptive to a dog's life - chaos, noise, screaming, crying, inane giggling, throwing plates onto the floor (and that's just the big humans cleaning up after them!) No, the grandchildren themselves will be just as bad, if not worse. Running around the house and garden and stealing all of your toys. Sometimes they will have a very little one that will mimic you cruelly by crawling around on all fours, threatening to steal your food from your bowl and invading your sanctuary under the dining table!

Not that children aren't great fun at times. They can be our best friends - playing sticks in the garden or letting us

120

into the secret dens they build beneath the stairs or outside behind the shed. On occasions they drop food for us to clean up or even give us treats secretly under the table when they don't want the humans to know they haven't eaten it. No we dogs have nothing against children per se, it's just that they rush about making loud noises and generally disrupt the routine of us totally being the centre of attention.

Now we have a duty to appear protective to these small bundles of energy and noise. It is expected that we boldly keep them safe from predators and strangers. When they arrive, grab the nearest toy and, keeping it firmly in your mouth patrol round and round the room, shaking it at them or pushing it into their legs, but don't actually let them take it from you. You, on the other hand, can steal their toys with impunity. The humans will just think it sweet that you are playing with the little ones. Steal the teddy and shake the stuffing out of him, while the child is screaming at you and chasing you he will get the blame for teasing you. This means that, while he is on the 'naughty step', you can raid his sweet bag and eat all of the jelly babies! This is a really good service since too much sugar will cause them tooth decay. Even if your boisterous play and interest in his sweets makes him cry, you can always win their hearts over at the end of the visit. Having worn the little people out, it is your duty to curl up with them on your day bed under the table. Cuddling them and letting them share your toys will soon render them sleepy and the humans cannot resist the sight of young toddlers and dogs cuddled together asleep. This should earn you bonus points and the odd biscuit bone or two once they go home and peace is restored. Well, until next weekend at least!

Your affectionate Uncle

Grufferty.

My Dear Nephew Tyson,

The matter of visitors and the art of jumping up

Every so often the humans will have strangers coming to the house. Sometimes these are friends greeted enthusiastically by your humans and others are on a far more formal footing. No matter what, you must greet them in your own way (which I will explain) and make your presence known.

If these are friends the chances are that you will have met them before and may even see them on a regular basis. This gives you endless possibilities for fun. It is vital that you show them how pleased you are to see them. The minute they ring the doorbell, fling yourself crazily and heavily against the front door barking ferociously the while. Once the door is opened to admit them, jump up at them smiling and huffing right in their faces. If you can arrange to eat something smelly and disgusting in the garden first, then your breath will have an even greater impact. If there is a lady amongst them wearing a skirt, it is imperative that, having huffed in her face, you then whip round behind her and stick your head up her skirt, cold nose foremost! This may cause your banishment to the kitchen for a while, but believe me, my boy, it will have been worth it!

Once they have been safely delivered to the sitting room, grab the most disreputable, smelly toy and run circuits of the room with it in your mouth shaking it the while and thrusting it into the shins of the visitors. This tactic must be repeated every time you cease to be the centre of attention. If the visitors are particularly fond of dogs, they may play with you for a while. Once they lose interest, lay at their feet on your back, legs in the air and look lovingly at them lips parted and jowls falling back in a clownish way. This will, 99% of the time, guarantee you much adoration and a pleasant tummy tickle from said visitors.

On some special occasions, the guests may be invited to dinner. This will mean that soon after your tummy tickle, they will all decamp to the dining room. It is VITAL that you slink in unnoticed and hide under the table before your human can evict you and banish you to the kitchen. Now if you have been fortunate enough to gain the affection of one of the guests, the one who tickled your tummy, (usually the female of the species) aim for their legs under the table and sit lightly on their feet pressed firmly up against their legs. This will ensure her undying affection, meaning she will not snitch on your presence in the room to your humans and she may even sneak bits of food under the table to you if it does not meet with her approval - a mutually satisfying agreement.

Once the meal is over and everyone rises to return to the sitting room, start the whole jumping up and huffing process again. It may be exhausting but it is well worth it.

It may be that the visitor is of the more formal type - the vicar, the double glazing salesman or the financial adviser. This being the case, it is imperative that you jump up and down barking hysterically to show what a good guard dog you are. Position yourself as close to them as you can once they have been seated and watch them like a hawk! Let them know you have counted the silver teaspoons and emit the occasional low growl never taking your eyes off them. This will ensure a speedy visit and, perhaps, prevent a second one. This means that you can get back to sleeping in your human's favourite armchair that much the sooner. Do not forget to repeat the jumping and hysterical barking when they get up to leave. It is also in the contract!

Your affectionate Uncle
Grufferty

My Dear Nephew Tyson

Vets and how to avoid them

You will, no doubt, at some time in the duration of your sojourn on earth, be taken to a place called the vets (or perhaps the two legged ones will call it the V. E. T .S. spelt out phonetically as if you were unable to spell.) It is rarely as bad as you think it is going to be, and quite often you come out feeling much better; but we have all heard the rumours. How Towser, the German Shepherd from three doors down, went in to have his claws clipped and came out minus two very important pieces of reproductive equipment. Or the horror story of Prince the Boxer from Jubilee Street who went in for worming pills and came out wearing the lampshade of shame and embarrassment around his neck! Now, I know that your Cousin Angus told you on your last visit with your family, that he was taken to his local Vet and, no sooner had he been lifted onto the examination table, than the two legged demon with the degree from the RVC and the gloves grabbed his bottom and squeezed it so hard that his eyes watered! (Angus' eyes, not the vets; although his watered a little afterwards when Angus bit him just at the top of his thigh!)

This, however, does not mean that you have to put up with the same fate. The two legged ones are very sly. They know that you will object, so they try to disguise it by pretending that you are going on an adventure, maybe to the woods for extra stick throwing. Watch and listen for the subtle signs. They will be extra sugary, smiling more sweetly than usual and keener to get you into the crate in the car. Time to employ the method discussed in my letter on the art of travel. This may not work very well, however, as the journey will usually not be a very long one. Plan B – Once in the hated car park at the vet, refuse to come out of the car. This will only be a delaying tactic as they will soon manhandle you out but it will create a diversion. Hang back reluctantly so that they have to drag you on the lead through the door. Once through the hated door, howl and whine at the top of your voice. Make sure to growl at every other animal you meet in the waiting room. Any old friend you know from the park will understand and will most probably be using these tactics themselves, which will add to the alarm and despondency.

You will doubtless meet new friends in the waiting room. The Lurcher from Coronation Gardens called 'Getdowndamndog' and the Bishon Friese from Acacia

Avenue called 'Shutupthatrow'. It is accepted that, even though you would get on fine if you met occasionally in the woods, today you eye each other suspiciously and growl menacingly. It adds to the human's stress levels and nervousness.

The final stage, when your name is called, is to howl hysterically and roll on the floor, eyes heavenward. This is guaranteed to cost the humans extra on the bill as it will be assumed you are having a seizure (with all the extra investigative tests involved.) Should you find yourself on the hated examination table anyway, summon up as much anger as your usual despondent self can and bite the vet! Imagine he is that squeaky floppy furry toy that they got you from Pets R Smart. Really sharpen those teeth and sink them into the softest bit of unprotected vet that you can find. This is a dead certainty to put the cost of your visit to the humans up by several pounds thus ensuring that you only really have to go when things are really bad, then, with a bit of luck, it will be a weekend and the cost will be double, as the vet will have to come to your house

Don't forget to employ the art of sulking all the way home and for several days after the visit. This should restrict the number of trips to the vet you have to make.

Your affectionate Uncle

Grufferty.

My dear Nephew Tyson

Cat flaps and How to master them

As you go through life with the humans, they may get (or take you to somewhere that has) a cat! I know that you will be well aware that we dogs stand no chance against such ninja warriors from hell! Be sure to creep around them and keep the peace (and under NO circumstances make eye contact). If you are lucky, there may be a cat flap. This presents endless possibilities for fun. Said cat flap will be in the bottom half of an outer door, usually the back one to the garden. This is fun anyway, but far greater fun if there are small humans, known as children, around.

Wait until all the two legged ones are distracted - a meal time is a good time. Just as they have sat at table to eat commence a hideous howl and scratch at the back door. This will cause mutterings and apologies from the humans but they will let you outside to answer the (assumed) call of nature. Listen very carefully! It is vital that you sniff about and wander aimlessly around the garden. Every so often make as if to crouch down then look accusingly at the human. Under NO circumstances should you answer any call of nature whatsoever. This should ensure that the human goes in and leaves you some privacy for a few minutes. Give them time to settle back in their seat, perhaps even as long as thirty seconds, then run and try to jump through the cat flap! I hasten to add that this will only be effective with medium sized breeds and upwards. Toys and miniature breeds need not bother - they will probably have been duffed up by the cat anyway by now! Of course, for this to work properly, you must be bigger than the perimeter of the cat flap. With any luck you will wedge firmly in the flap, unable to budge either into the house or back out again into the garden. For maximum effect make sure that the little ones, if any are present, are in the garden with you and cannot, therefore, get back in. This will have the double effect of stressing the humans to the maximum and teaching the little ones how to get their heads stuck in the cat flap at a future date.

In the ensuring panic and alarm, they will doubtless remove the whole frame of the cat flap and maybe even cut a bigger hole in the door. Once this has been achieved, turn your head diagonally across the frame and pull it out backwards, then calmly walk away from the door into the house. For extra bonus points, if there is still any dinner on the table, be sure to steal it while the humans are otherwise engaged, thus ensuring you never have to visit, or see those visitors again.

Wishing you every success with this venture

Your affectionate Uncle

Grufferty

My Dear Nephew Tyson,

Sticks and how to use them

I am quite sure by now, you must be familiar with the game beloved of the humans called sticks. This usually involves being dragged around the park or woods and having wooden sticks thrown amazing distances by the two legged ones who then expect you to dash off after said stick and bring it back to them. They seem to delight in this totally pointless exercise. It may be that you have, in the past, indulged them in this. Wagging your tail and bouncing furiously around their legs as they take aim, then bounding after it grinning madly and bringing it back, only to have to do the whole pointless thing again to cries of "Good boy! Clever dog!" and suchlike. Has it never occurred to you that you are doing all the work here? They are strolling along maybe as much as half a mile while you leap about and dash off covering three times the distance they do and expending far more energy than is needed just to please them.

Think again! There is a much more fun way of playing this game! Wait until they find a juicy stick and throw it, then ignore them totally. Sniff around a bit, find a tree to investigate but do NOT I repeat NOT chase that stick. This will confuse them. They will try to encourage you by pointing madly and shouting with evermore urgency "Fetch! Come on, boy – FETCH it". Ignore them, grin and huff at them wagging your tail madly and looking at the stick, but do not chase it. They will eventually go and get it themselves and shake it at you before throwing it again. If you stick by your guns (pun intended) and wait patiently, they may repeat the process thus covering almost as much ground as you have.

After a while they will get the message and, with some disappointment, will give up. This is the time to find a stick and shake it at them, pushing it painfully into their shins and bouncing around enthusiastically. Listen carefully to this next bit. The human will take the stick from you and throw it with encouraging words such as "Fetch it, boy!" Be sure to Jump up and intercept it in mid-air, then, shaking it, crunch it up into hundreds of little pieces and spit them out. Repeat this exercise until the human loses interest.

Just before you leave the woods or park, find a huge branch - at least three times as wide as yourself, and much wider than the car door or the door of the house. Hold it lovingly in your jaws (even though the weight is killing you) and refuse to part with it - refuse totally to leave without it and try your hardest to get it into the car. It is vital that you do not succeed in this, leave it to your human. Stick to your guns (another pun intended); this will cause maximum difficulty to your human as they will have to use all sorts of ingenuity to get it into the car and home. Once they carry it from the car into the back garden and place it lovingly on the lawn for you, refuse absolutely to have anything whatsoever to do with it ever again.

This can all be repeated on future walks to maximise the fun. I look forward to hearing about it in your next letter.

Your affectionate Uncle
Grufferty

The next, and final, e-mail was short but enlightening ....

My Dear Nephew Tyson

This is just a quick line as I have to finish my speech for the Wings Awards ceremony to welcome the new arrivals!

Today we had a new arrival from your side of the bridge - a small Pomeranian called Probate. He was looking for his deceased human, a solicitor from a small place called England. I had to break it to him gently that there were no solicitors on this side of the rainbow bridge. They, along with all politicians, terrorists, bankers, estate agents and traffic wardens, murderers and a luke warm pottage of adulterers and hypocrites, had gone to the other place, under the bridge where perpetual fireworks, thunder and the dreaded vacuum cleaner reign supreme.

In the centre of this noisome hole, where eternal bonfires burn, gunshot is constant and firecrackers crash, are the child and animal abusers - the worst of the bunch. They are doomed until eternity to have their flesh torn by claws, their buttocks bitten and their shins gnawed by Cerebos the terrible two headed avenging canine angel.

Let this serve as a warning to all the humans; love and cherish your four legged, winged, furry, feathered, finned and reptilian friends!

Your affectionate Uncle
Grufferty

Grufferty Proposes a Toast

The scene is set at the Wings Ceremony for new arrivals of the Worshipful Order of Canine's residing over the Rainbow Bridge. The Bridge Keeper has asked Grufferty, a very senior canine angel, to give the after dinner speech. Here it is reproduced in its entirety for our edification

My most worshipful Keeper, lords, bitches, curs, mutts and gentle-dogs!

It has fallen as my lot this year, to have the honour of addressing our most eminent gathering on this, the occasion of our Wings awards dinner. It is a duty that I am proud to perform. Our worshipful Keeper has to attend many of these meetings each year for every species over the bridge, so I will keep this brief. It is many centuries, in earthly time, that I have been attending this annual meeting and in that time I have seen many changes both in standards and attitudes of our dependents, the humans, down below the Bridge on Earth. I know that every generation says the same of the new recruits, but, really, the rookies of today have every opportunity and a bright future before them. Things were very different in my day!

There was a time, long ago, when humans were to be respected. They gave us shelter, food and companionship. In return we hunted for them, retrieved, guarded their caves and kept the hyenas at bay. We rubbed along with mutual respect and both had something to offer the other. That was a time when man was judged, not by his birth, wealth, social standing, or whether he wore a designer suit, but by his actions, deeds and kindness to others; above all, to us, his best friend. Each man had a role in life, much as we dogs did. Man provided for his family. He worked as a hunter gatherer or ruled or governed the country, overseeing his lands or scribing in an office, tilling his land or the land of his master, all to provide for his family and dogs. Each man knew his place in the world. He popped into the local inn for his ale on his way home from the fields (or his office) in the evening. Some of us were lucky enough to spend the day in the fields helping our masters. We could accompany him to the local tavern and sit dreamily under the table whilst he smoked his pipe and shared a yarn with his cronies before returning home. Some of us would be taken out for walkies on his return before supper and bed. When he was worried or needed advice there was either the Vicar, or the Squire to help him. A walk up to the Manor or the Vicarage, cap in hand; a chat with the Reverend or Guv'nor and, half an hour later, back to the cottage with a spring in his step and a clearer mind, his future course set before him.

Woman! She knew her place too, She was gentle, tender and kind; feeding her babies and washing the laundry, cooking and cleaning the cottage or keeping her husband happy. If she were of a certain social standing, she spent her time, overseeing the servants, visiting the cottages of her husband's estate workers, or taking part in various charitable works to ease the burden of those less fortunate. If her standing were not high, she would work in the big house or help bring in the harvest from the fields, baby on hip and toddler helping to pick the crop. Her role was to bring comfort and reassurance to her family and to tend their needs - soothing the spouse's fevered brow or kissing better the scraped knees of her offspring.

If not helping in the fields rounding sheep or fetching the game from the shoot, we could always lie companionably by the kitchen range looking protectively over the missus and her little ones (and catching the odd tasty morsel from the cooking pot.)

Life continued in this vein for centuries, peaceful, unhurried and certain. Then, just after the turn of the twentieth century, the storm clouds gathered and broke in the form of a huge world war. Life changed forever. Man proved just how hateful and treacherous he could be, not to mention how downright stupid. The wicked waste of lives, a whole generation of young men decimated, women widowed and children orphaned.

Women learnt to drive the ambulances and army vehicles. Some opened up their big houses to take in the injured troops returning home. They nursed and kept the home ready in the fervent hope that their men would be amongst the lucky ones who returned home to their farms and homesteads.

We did our bit along with rank upon rank of our cousins here, the horses. Many of us were sacrificed, but it seemed as if the humans were on the path to extinction. Finally the dust settled. They took up the broken threads of life and carried on until, a little over a quarter of a century later, they proved that they had learnt nothing and it all started again!

In times of adversity, mankind is driven to greater levels of inventiveness and resource. This time the second world conflagration was ended when, in his brilliance, mankind invented a weapon that could cause mass destruction - even, in the wrong hands, the destruction of the whole of Earth!

The sands were shifting. The weather vane of destiny swung round to point in our direction, Mankind was in the final stages of his self-destruction. It was time for dogs everywhere to mobilise and prepare for the takeover of the world. This was when the early seeds of our mission to seize control and rule the Earth were sown. The power lay in our own paws!

The main change wrought by this terrible war was the independence of woman. With the men away fighting, women had to take on many of the roles traditionally filled by men. Once more they farmed, drove vehicles and worked in factories but many found that, not only did the new jobs pay more, but they loved the newfound freedom and independence gained by them. Women had found their forte! They realised that they could manage without the need to commit themselves to a man. They mistook this new emancipation for power! They thought that they were clever. There was no longer a need to prostitute themselves to marriage for a living; they could do it for themselves! Us wise ones know that true power and strength lies in captivating a man with true womanly wiles. Beauty, sensuality, love and devotion to the family will cause any good man to bow to his woman's will and do anything for her - even facing death itself! The real power lies in being there behind your man, influencing his thoughts and actions in a way so subtle that he thinks it all his own doing. These 'modern women' mistook those female virtues for weakness. They wanted total equality, to dress like men, drink like men, swear like men. Some of them went to war like men, even loved like men and partnered each other.

The natural reaction was inevitable. As women became more independent, men became emasculated. Many of them swapped roles with their women, sending them out to work while they stayed at home caring for the children. Chivalry died forever. No more giving up seats on trains or walking on the outside of the pavement when walking with the woman. Some even expected their female partners (no one bothered to marry anymore) to cook and clean too when they got back from their day jobs. Modern emancipated women had scored an own goal! Men became as women and vice versa and the whole of humanity became a watered down soup of ambiguous beings of indeterminate sexuality. The up side to this is the tolerance and acceptance that goes with these changes, but it is all topsy turvey. Happily it became unacceptable to judge people by the colour of their skin, their race or their religion, but often the pendulum swung too much in the other direction. Some Americans raged through the streets shooting and killing the police in an imagined revenge for perceived police brutality. The criminal became the hero, the lawmen became public enemies. Any difference of political opinion from the masses was met, not with interest, but with derision and insults. Human society praised people for parading their sexuality abroad, becoming a reality TV star or earning vast sums for kicking a football around a field while ignoring the heroes who save lives or rage war against criminals and gangsters. All religions were, quite rightly tolerated, but sometimes those very religions brought their own laws that made it acceptable to kill someone for their sexual orientation, of murder their sisters or daughters if they pursued an education or dressed in a foreign fashion. People would fete a celebrity whilst attacking a paramedic trying to do his job on a Saturday night. Sportsmen and women were given a far higher salary than their worth (more than top surgeons saving lives or pioneering scientists). The Vicar is now female and her role is largely voluntary, no 'livings' to be gotten from the church nowadays. The Squire has been deposed by the peasants. It has become a sin to be born into any kind of wealth or to have a private education - everything became acceptable except being born into wealth or title. Such people became public enemy number one and open to every abuse and ridicule. The 'noblesse oblige' that came with the Squire's role has now been replaced with the Jobcentre where, instead of a half an hour chat with the Squire, they queue for hours reading a tacky tabloid newspaper while their fellow unemployed swear at and threaten the staff as each man believes the world owes them a living. The person flipping burgers in a restaurant demands to earn the same hourly rate as a peace keeping soldier stationed miles away from his (or her) family or a trained nurse manning the monitors in the Intensive care unit! He believes it is society's job to support him and his family!

These changes were inevitable for any race that destroys its own habitat. The writing was on the wall with the extinction of the Dodo! Man has destroyed the rainforests, built over valuable farming land. Many species have been hunted to extinction, the logical and inevitable conclusion to this is the self- destruction of mankind completely!

We, of course, have taken advantage of this. We have educated ourselves by observing them. Our mission to seize control of Earth is well underway. We can push ourselves forward as a fashion accessory. We no longer have cross breeds or mongrels, we have Labradoodles, Chihaucollies, Cockapoos and Doberwhilers and Bull terriers crossed with Shih Tzu's! The more vicious we look (of course we are softies really) the better they like to show us off. It does mean we can rule the roost at home. Where once we slept in front of the kitchen range if we were lucky (the barn if not) now we sleep on the best sofa, or even on their bed with them. We are dressed in sparkling collars and coats of the finest material. Some of us are permanently carried around in designer handbags, clutched against silicone implanted breasts bulging under expensive designer clothing.

Mankind has become impotent, bent on destroying itself. They kill each other; man, woman and child regardless. They maim and torture, all in the name of religion, what do they know of God? The Keeper of the Bridge? Are they really on His side? They are so far away from any truth or hope of life in the hereafter. We are now in a wonderful position to take over the reins of the world. Even without an opposable thumb, we cannot make a bigger hash of things than they have done. They cannot see that any race that vilifies it's educated and more wealthy sectors while expecting society to provide for them, will soon self -destruct as the wealth runs out. We are now educated, perhaps far more so than mankind. We are naturally kind, with an inbuilt duty to care and nurture those weaker than ourselves. We are faithful and loving. This is the stage we are now at, my fellow canines, the hands of time stand at five to midnight and, on the first stroke, we will swoop. We will lead the world, the remnants of mankind will bow to our will and the world will once more be a happy place, full of love and hope for a brighter future. Mankind will be no more and all the animals, led by us dogs, will reign supreme. We must all prepare, the time draws nigh.

Tonight we send you new recruits forth, to watch over mankind and wait your chance. Here we have partaken of a most delicious sumptuous feast of the finest chicken and marrowbones. The future world we create will be even more delicious and fulfilling. My most worshipful Keeper, lords, bitches, curs, mutts and gentle dogs, please raise your water bowls and join me in a toast to our great mission for our future – I have seen the future and we will **S**eize **C**ontrol and **R**ule of **E**arth and the **W**orld by **E**ducated **D**ogs - I give you the future and the future is - **SCREWED** – Cheers!

Also available by the same author

- Traders of the Fifth Continent – Tales of Smugglers and Rascals on the Romney Marsh (March 2015)   available at £5
- The Dark Lantern (and other Tales)
  19 short stories on a variety of subjects.
  (July 2016)   available at £6
- Sister at the Sharp End – Nursing Experiences from the 1970s and 1980s
  (August 2018)   available at £7
- Enter at A and other Tales of Terror – handy tips for the Dressage Rookie
  (November 2018   available at £5

These are available from WattKnott Publishing
Testers, Whatlington, Battle, East Sussex TN33 0NS
Or email: lyncharliewatts@hotmail.co.uk

Prices include postage and packing
All are available from Ebay or Amazon

The first 3 books are also available on Kindle